Here is the full account of the blazing courage
and dogged resolution of the men who, in
1942, manned 'the bravest and most fateful of
all the convoys that were ever sailed to relieve
Malta'.

An armada of two battleships, four aircraft
carriers, twelve cruisers and forty destroyers
was deployed to escort and protect fourteen
merchant ships. Ranged against them were
twenty-one submarines, twenty-three E-boats
and five hundred and forty aircraft.

One of the five merchantmen who survived
to reach Malta was the tanker *Ohio*, whose
name has passed into history.

The central theme of this book is the fantas-
tic story of the men who sailed and fought in
her, refusing to consider defeat; and of the ship
herself who, broken-backed and sinking, carried the oil which was Malta's sole hope of
survival.

PETER SHANKLAND and
ANTHONY HUNTER

Malta Convoy

FONTANA/Collins

First published 1961
First issued in Fontana Books 1963
Ninth impression June 1989

© Peter Shankland & Anthony Hunter 1961

Printed and bound in Great Britain by
Caledonian International Book Manufacturing Ltd, Glasgow

TO THE MEMORY
OF ALL WHO WERE LOST
AT SEA
1939–1945

CONTENTS

AUTHORS' PREFACE

This book is meant to picture as vividly as possible the drama of a great naval action, to recreate as it happened what is now accepted as one of the most vital convoys of the war.

It is also essentially a reappraisal of the facts.

The jigsaw of grand strategy has been fitted together, leaders on both sides have opened their war diaries, and in the light of later knowledge much that was obscure in 1942 is now clear.

In telling this story we have had all viewpoints, official and unofficial, Allied and Axis, before us. A large number of men of all ranks who served in Operation Pedestal have described their experiences afresh. But when attempting to reproduce full and accurate detail of a naval action, it is inevitable that conflict of evidence should occur. In a few places we have had to use our own judgement. For instance, in the later stages of Operation Pedestal the men were so tired that their recollections of the fast-changing scene of battle were often blurred or inaccurate when they came to write their official reports. In all such cases we have plotted the situation in detail, arriving at a final conclusion only from the evidence before us.

The story centres round the fortunes of the tanker *Ohio*. We chose her as our main theme because she was the last to arrive at her destination, and because, being the only tanker, she was probably the most important ship in the convoy. Her fight to Malta has an epic quality and epitomises the best wartime tradition of British seamanship. Some of the volunteers, naval officers and ratings and merchant seamen, who manned her guns and handled her towlines on the last stage of her long voyage, were American. It can now be seen that the survival of Malta, perhaps that of the free world itself, depended on the endurance of her small British crew, these volunteers who came to her assistance, and on the stoutness of this American ship's construction.

Our thanks are due to the British Admiralty, without whose close co-operation and unfailing aid this book would have been impossible. All official documents relating to the action were placed at our disposal, and the courtesy, skill and assistance received from experts in the Historical Records, Foreign Documents, Film and Photographic and other departments helped immeasurably with the many difficult research problems.

Our thanks are also due to the many survivors of the action who helped us with personal accounts, in particular to Captain Dudley Mason, GC, of *Ohio* and his Chief Engineer Jimmy Wyld, DSO, Admiral Sir Harold Burrough, GCB, KBE, DSO, commander of the convoy close escort, who also allowed us to include two of his personal photographs, and to Sir Edward St John Jackson, KCMG, KBE, the Deputy Governor of Malta in 1942, and many other officials and heads of departments in many services.

Much invaluable aid was also received from: Central Office of Information, *Daily Mail*, Eagle Oil Company, *Evening News*, Imperial War Museum, Ministry of Transport, Movietone News, the Royal Air Force, Sun Shipbuilding Company of USA, *Sunday Dispatch*, Texas Oil Company of USA, US Department of Commerce, and the War Office. Grateful acknowledgement is made to Captain E. W. Roskill, RN and Messrs Collins, who permitted us to reproduce the map of Operation Pedestal from *The Navy at War* 1934–45.

PETER SHANKLAND
ANTHONY HUNTER

FOREWORD
by
ADMIRAL OF THE FLEET
SIR PHILIP VIAN
GCB, KBE, DSO

This is the story of the bravest and most fateful of all
the convoys that were ever sailed to relieve Malta in the
late war.

The operation was called Pedestal, and it was
mounted in August 1942, at a time when the Governor
of the Island was faced with capitulation in a matter of
days.

Survival from a disaster whose magnitude was not
easily calculable depended on the delivery in quantity of
two commodities: food and fuel. Provisioning of the
fortress could achieve no useful military purpose unless
aircraft and warships based on the Island received the
fuel necessary to enable them to continue their operations against the enemy supply line to Africa.

Pedestal began in the knowledge that the Axis powers
were fully informed of the plan, and that they had made
dispositions for every possible form of attack with which
to destroy the convoy in its protracted passage.

The naval forces based at Alexandria usually referred
to Gibraltar as the 'Ladies End' of the Mediterranean, a
reflection on the security from bombing of the harbour
itself, and the freedom from attack by heavy surface
ships almost always enjoyed by the Gibraltar-Malta
convoys. The detailed description in this book of the
passage of Pedestal has caused me to regard the soubri-
quet as wrong, for it is hard to conceive conditions

demanding greater fortitude, endurance and sacrifice than was undergone by the officers and men of this convoy and its escort as, in ever-diminishing numbers, way was made eastward to Malta.

As the operation drew towards its spell-binding end, the preservation of Malta from the dreaded capitulation rested on two factors. The first was intervention by Italian surface forces in the waters south of Sicily, whose attack the decimated escort could have had no chance of defeating. The second concerned a ship, the American-built tanker *Ohio*, famous, fabulous, never to be forgotten, and the centre-piece of the book. Broken-backed, near awash, without propulsion or the power of steam, could she be got into the Grand Harbour to discharge her miraculously preserved cargo of oil into the Island's empty tanks?

Success depended as much on the construction of the ship as on the continued endurance and valour of Captain Mason and his crew, and on the ability of the young officers commanding a handful of tiny warships to achieve, in face of enemy air opposition, a feat of towing which was for them unimaginable by any reasonable standard.

The reader is in fact presented with a story of greatness; great in the impact of the operation on history, great as a description of conflict at sea, and greatest as a study of sacrifice and endurance, with absolute refusal to accept defeat. By its very nature drama succeeds drama as the narrative unfolds. It would have been easy for the authors to indulge in melodrama; but this they have rightly avoided.

The fighting, point and counterpoint, which accompanied the greater part of the voyage is vividly and objectively described; while in recapturing the atmosphere both in the ships, as casualty followed casualty, and in Malta itself, which only the arrival of ships could preserve, the temptation has been resisted to introduce the writers' own emotions and opinions, for which they

would have had ample justification; for Shankland was
a Lieutenant RNVR in HMS *Speedy*, which played a
conspicuous part in the final stages of *Ohio*'s voyage,
while Hunter was a Spitfire pilot. With this background,
and by having been at pains to interview many of the
survivors of the operation, they have produced a narrative which breathes, and is authentic.

As one reads, heroes emerge. In addition to Captain
Mason of the *Ohio*, and many other merchant seamen,
my heart, as a naval officer, goes out to Rear-Admiral
Burrough, presented with a succession of crises, yet
never wavering; and to Commander Hill of HMS *Ledbury*, whose intrepidity and resource seemed to have no
limit.

The authors refer to Nelson's blockade of Malta in
the years 1798–1800, when Valletta – which had been
seized by Bonaparte on his way to Egypt – was held for
the French by the brave Vaubois. The garrison then
faced a hostile population, and a British fleet which,
after the victory of the Nile, was predominant in the
Mediterranean.

The French found Malta costly just as we did in World
War II. They lost the only two ships of the line which
managed to elude Nelson at Aboukir Bay, both when
trying to run the gauntlet from Malta to the safety of
their home shores. And Vaubois had to surrender, in the
end, because he could not get sea-borne supplies. Even
one merchant ship, fully laden, would have made all the
difference at the most critical time. It is true indeed
that, if history never quite repeats itself, it affords
endless and fascinating parallels.

'If ever students should seek an example of the
costliness in war of failure by a maritime power to
defend its overseas bases in peace,' writes Captain
Roskill in *The War at Sea*, 'the story of Malta's ordeal
in 1942 will provide the classic case.' That ordeal
was matched in the ships endeavouring to supply the
Island.

PROLOGUE

The launching of a ship, be she twelve-foot dinghy, ocean-going liner or great battleship, is a solemn occasion.

At this moment the future looms nearer unseen but not unfelt; and pride of workmanship becomes humbled before the immensity of the challenge to mighty elements and a fate beyond man's control.

Man-the-Builder has toiled for days, months or even years to shape this new and shining tool. Now it is to be committed to the sea, to a hidden destiny; and Man-the-Seafarer must put forth in her to test the mystery of oceans and to give her the life for which she has been cunningly made.

No one can tell if that life will be short or long, a maiden voyage wreck or years of tramping the seas to an honourable discharge in the shipbreaker's yard. Men die for her or because of her, others may become rich or ruined through her and great issues may hang upon the seamanship of her crew or the strength of her keel.

Such a moment of veiled truth fell on the dusty shipyards at Chester, Pennsylvania, on the morning of 20 April 1940. A ship was about to be born and already some of the chocks had been knocked away. Her rudder was secured for the launch and a web of preventer cables had been reeved to restrain her complete escape from the land.

A wooden platform, decked in red and white canvas for the ceremony, stood like a matchbox beneath the towering bows.

Nearby, groups of workmen stood gazing up at her, dressed in their best Sunday clothes for the occasion. Among them were shipwrights, riveters, carpenters,

welders, steel-cutters and the host of other craftsmen
whose hands and tools had helped to shape the broad
hull and the intricate vitals of what was about to become
one of the most modern oil tankers in the world.

An air of expectancy and the satisfaction of work well
done damped down the conversation, reducing it to
disjointed small talk. Unconsciously, the future pos-
sessed these men, as it was shortly to possess their
handiwork. For the last time they contemplated the
embodiment of a mystery – the fine artefact, assembled
from disordered masses of common raw material, which
had somehow become unified and beautiful in the
process.

To the knowledgeable, Hull 190 was doubly beautiful.
Looking at those bows where the neat white numbers of
the lading gauge measured off the underwater hull, she
was a skilful compromise, promising broad cargo-carry-
ing capacity to the profit-minded merchant and the
shapeliness of speed, the balance of stability, to the
mariner. Above the waterline, she was both roman-
tically and historically interesting: for the cutwater
soared in the graceful outward curve of a schooner bow,
which bore the now almost forgotten influence of the
old American clipper ship, carrying with it the legend of
wool and grain races and the fury of Cape Horn seas.

Towering above the little men below, it seemed that
she had overgrown them and was on the point of
bursting out of the steel slipway gantries which confined
her like a womb.

Below in the shipyard, uneasiness had replaced this
mixture of satisfaction and futurity. The advertised time
for the launching had come and gone, but the ceremonial
platform remained empty.

Eyes began to turn towards the water and heads were
shaken; for the usually placid current of the River
Delaware was whipped by a rising north-easterly gale,
and lumpy waves beat heavily on the tail of No. 2
Slipway.

In the main office of the Sun Shipbuilding Company, a neat white building almost lost among the ribs of partly-built ships and the organized confusion of the shipyard, a hurried conference was in progress.

On the table lay the familiar emblems of a launch: the bouquet and the bottle of champagne; and while the men present talked of technicalities, the prospective sponsor of Hull 190, Mrs Florence E. Rodgers, from Columbus, Ohio, stared out of the window at the wind-blown clouds.

The President of the Texas Oil Company crossed the room: 'It's no good, Mother. We'll have to postpone the launch. It's too much of a risk in this wind,' he said regretfully.

Mrs Rodgers was disappointed. 'What a shame. Isn't it supposed to be unlucky . . .?'

There was a second's hesitation, the realization of unspoken, subliminal thought, and then the ship-men were quick to assure her and themselves. That was just superstition . . . old-fashioned . . . after all no one could control the weather.

Outside it seemed evident that the waters were unwilling to receive the new ship. A full gale whistled through the gantries and howled about the crane jibs. The River Delaware was flecked with white, breaking waves.

Down by Slipway No. 2, the yard manager broke the news to the waiting men, and some of them were in no doubt about the significance of this omen.

'No good will come of it,' said one shipwright, shaking his pipe in the air. 'Better a busted stern than a late launch. It's unlucky.' Many of the men nodded their heads.

It is doubtful whether anyone present connected this unlucky omen with the faint rumblings from across the Atlantic, where the 'phoney war' in Europe was about to blaze up in the German invasion of France.

No one could have guessed then that the fate of this fine ship, built for the tanker fleet of 'Texaco', America's largest oil company, was bound up in that struggle, as America's own fate would be before two years were past.

To the average American the war seemed very far off then and would remain one of those things which only happen elsewhere for some time to come; but wiser and more forward-looking men had already measured the menace of Germany's ambitions and the rising threat of military preparations in Japan. Indeed, their forebodings had affected the building plan of Hull 190.

Laid down on 7 September 1939, four days after Germany had gone to war with Britain and France, the ship had been completed in the unusually short period of seven months, fifteen days.

Similarly, the approach of war had influenced her design, for unofficial conversations between military and oil chiefs had resulted in a ship of 9,263 tons, 515 feet in overall length, and capable of carrying 170,000 barrels of oil, bigger and more capacious than any tanker built before.

The Westinghouse turbine engines, which were shortly to be lowered into her, developed 9,000 shaft horsepower at ninety revolutions a minute which was calculated to drive the ship along at sixteen knots, a speed never attained before by a single screw tanker.

In this, America was guarding against the possibility of war in the Pacific, where large, swift oil tankers might one day have to carry, over vast distances, the life-blood of her fleets and armies.

Her method of construction was controversial. For some years the pros and cons of riveting versus welding ships had raged on both sides of the Atlantic. Hull 190, with a bottom shell and deck of the new-fashioned welded construction, was fated to settle once and for all the reliability of this method.

A composite framing system with two longitudinally continuous bulkheads, divided the ship into twenty-one cargo tanks, and this was designed to make her literally a honeycomb of strength.

These things, and many other uncommon fitments, were dictated by a growing fear of war, and this ship, which fate seemed unwilling to receive into her natural element was, in aggregate, much more than a mere tanker made to plough the peaceful waters of the Gulf of Mexico.

The day following that scheduled for her launch was no less depressing. Unfriendly skies darkened the shipyard. A grey, continuous rain was falling, but this had damped down the wind and the waters of the Delaware, though sullen and uninviting, were calm.

The launch proceeded. Swathed in raincoats, a small party huddled together under umbrellas on the platform. Mrs Rodgers grasped the bottle of champagne in her right hand and pronounced the words:

'I name this good ship *Ohio*. May God go with her and all who sail in her. Good luck . . .'

The bottle smashed against the bow, the launching button was pressed. For a moment there was no movement, then no more than a slight shudder. *Ohio* seemed reluctant to start upon her momentous journey.

At last she began to move slowly away from them, gathering speed on the greased slips, until she plunged with a roar of parting waters into the river.

A passing tug whistled forlornly, the shipyard siren shrilled and a thin cheer went up from the men who built her.

As she rode high and unballasted on the waters, who could have foretold the trial by fire, bomb and torpedo which was to test every plate of her in the far waters of the Mediterranean? Who could have foreseen the saga which she was to enact?

For the name *Ohio* was to be written in the roll of the world's great ships. The course of the war and the way of life in the Western world were to hang upon her strength and the courage of the men who were to sail in her.

CHAPTER ONE

Linchpin of the Hinge

*I now declare that I consider Malta as a most import-
ant outwork of India, that will ever give us great
influence in the Levant, and indeed all the southern
parts of Italy. In this view, I hope we shall never give
it up.*   LORD NELSON

*The interrelation between Malta and the Desert oper-
ations was never so plain as in 1942, and the heroic
defence of the Island in that year formed the keystone
of the prolonged struggle for the maintenance of our
position in Egypt and the Middle East.*
    WINSTON CHURCHILL

*Malta . . . has the lives of many thousands of German
and Italian soldiers on its conscience.*   ROMMEL

I

By August 1942, disaster had beset Britain in all theatres
of war. Everywhere the tide had set against her and it
seemed that she was losing the struggle for freedom.

Not that any Briton would have admitted it, far less
spoken of it, then. Life went on with a grumble or a
laugh much as it had always done, though the pinch of
hardship had already created great changes at home.

Food was short and the women queued daily, tender-
ing ration cards for a little meat, a little tea and a little
sugar.

Men and women had become accustomed to living
with imminent danger, and the unrelieved darkness of

the blackout, the ruined gaps in many neat rows of houses, were a constant reminder of the nearness of war.

These tribulations were accepted with a certain phlegmatic adaptability which at times of crisis belies the traditional conservatism of the British. Yet at no time since the days of Dunkirk and the Battle of Britain had the situation been blacker. The Allied armed forces had taken a beating in the familiar fields of France, in the Arctic cold of Norway, in the torrid heat of the Far East and finally on the temperate shores of the blue Mediterranean.

Everywhere the coils of the Axis seemed to be strangling the life out of every effort. An unceasing expenditure of blood, will and material had shown nothing but reverses and increase of difficulties; and even to the most optimistic it was plain that there could be no quick decision other than defeat with an alternative of long years of toil, turmoil and bereavement.

The British had been told that the air battle for Britain had been won, yet air-raid sirens still tried the nerves of the hardiest and sent the prudent to cold nights in the shelters. Searchlights probed the skies, guns crashed and night-fighters took off from their aerodromes; but still the raiders droned on, night after night, and dropped their bombs, for no means had so far been found to stop them.

From the outbreak of war the British had looked hopefully towards the Americans, feeling that these kinsmen of theirs would not finally desert them, and counting on their entry into the war to turn the tide of battle. Yet after the Americans had joined the Allies on 7 December 1941, there was no interruption in the train of disaster.

Winston Churchill, the Prime Minister, confided something of the bitter disappointment felt in a dispatch to his friend the American President, Franklin D. Roosevelt, in March 1942. 'When I reflect,' he wrote, 'how I have longed and prayed for the entry of the

United States into the war, I find it difficult to realize how gravely our British affairs have deteriorated by what has happened since December 7th.'

By August 1942, the British had suffered from the Japanese as badly as the Americans who, with many of their ships lying at the bottom of Pearl Harbour, could do little, it seemed, to counter the new menace.

To many it had been a severe psychological shock to discover that the little yellow man of the cartoons, with protruding teeth and a sword too big for him, had suddenly grown to the stature of a giant. He was no longer a character from a Gilbertian opera, but a determined and fanatical enemy, who had quickly proved that his weapons were newer and sharper than the quaint swords of his Samurai ancestors.

His armies had swept through the Malay Peninsula, brushing aside the British defence. His air force had sunk, within minutes, two battleships, *Repulse* and *Prince of Wales*, sent to protect Singapore, and as he closed in on that 'Impregnable Fortress', the key to British Far-Eastern possessions, the depressingly familiar tale of lack of AA defence, obsolete fighters, muddle and underestimation of the enemy soon began to filter back to Britain.

Armoured landing craft, marked with the Rising Sun, crossed the Singapore strait and, 30 hours later, 70,000 dazed and beaten men surrendered and passed into brutal captivity.

After the capture of Singapore, the Japanese pressed on with the speed of a forest fire. Java and Sumatra were occupied, and a heavy air-raid emphasized the threat to Australia. From invasion bases at Bangkok and Mergui in Thailand, they crossed the River Salween, intended as a major line of British defence, stormed into Rangoon, cut the lines of communication between the British army and its Chinese allies in the Shan Hills and by the end of May 1942 stood at the gates of India.

Keeping pace with their armies, the Japanese fleet

broke into the Indian Ocean, sank the carrier *Hermes*, 2 British cruisers and 112,312 tons of Allied shipping. Before the threat of the Japanese carriers the British Eastern Fleet, despite heavy reinforcement, was compelled to withdraw to East Africa, leaving the Japanese in undisputed control of the Indian Ocean. The invasion of Ceylon, as a prelude to the attack on India, seemed to be imminent.

The other great ally from whom so much had at first been expected had also failed to justify popular hopes. The Russian steam-roller had lumbered backwards and, with losses which boggled the imagination, the Red armies were fighting for their lives before Moscow and Stalingrad.

From the start of Hitler's invasion of their territory, the British War Cabinet had been at pains to help the Russians, but there was little they could do beyond sending the maximum amount of war material to make up for their appalling shortages of modern weapons and transport. Most of this material had to be convoyed through the Arctic Sea to Northern Russia. In these waters to fight nature was sufficiently arduous. In recurrent storms huge waves hammered the ships and left decks and upperworks dangerously top-heavy with deep coatings of ice. Gun mechanisms froze and frostbite depleted the crews. Pack-ice forced the convoys towards the coast of Norway, a route commanded by Axis aircraft and fleet units stationed in the fjords. The British, attacked almost unceasingly, sustained frightening losses both in ships and men, for no one could live long in the frozen sea.

In one convoy alone, PQ 17, which sailed for Murmansk in July, twenty-three out of thirty-six ships were lost.

Coming at a time when the Battle of the Atlantic had reached its height, when Britain's lifeline of supplies from America was in serious danger of becoming disrupted, and even severed completely, such losses were almost insupportable.

In the six months preceding that fateful August of 1942, German submarines had sunk 3,250,000 tons of British and Allied shipping alone, and the U-boat packs had already begun to appear on the American east coast where a further 100,000 tons a month were being sent to the bottom.

So it seemed that, in the world struggle to maintain the supply routes upon which Britain depended, the Allies were being beaten and as yet no remedy had been found.

Then, as if to underline the fear that British command of the sea was waning, the German battle-cruisers *Scharnhorst* and *Gneisenau* and the heavy cruiser *Prinz Eugen* steamed through the English Channel from Brest to Kiel, untouched except for slight damage caused by mines. That an enemy fleet could make free with Britain's own Channel without loss, for the first time since before the Spanish Armada, seemed to outrage the best traditions of a seafaring people.

At first the Mediterranean had offered the brightest prospects of a success for British arms. General Wavell had bundled the Italians out of Cyrenaica, and in the desert alone it had been possible to point to a theatre of war in which a great host of prisoners and great quantities of booty had been taken, besides vast areas of enemy territory. The scene quickly changed. A German general called Rommel, unknown then, had already begun to organize counter-measures. The Germans were also preparing to take a hand in the war in Greece where the Italian legions had made little headway against the determined resistance of a numerically inferior Greek army.

It was only when German Panzer groups were already moving through Bulgaria to attack them that the Greeks consented to accept British help, and four divisions were moved from North Africa to Greece leaving inadequate forces to maintain the desert front. When Rommel attacked with the newly-formed Afrika Korps, the British were compelled to fall back. Brilliantly exploiting the situation, the German general outflanked the opposing army and turned its withdrawal into a disorderly retreat. Only the failure to take Tobruk halted his advance on the borders of Egypt.

Meanwhile, the Greek disaster had begun. Unable to stem the German drive into Greece, and bombed relentlessly by overwhelmingly superior German air forces, the British army was withdrawn to Crete. Nor were the British given a breathing space there. Within a month, thousands of white parachutes mushroomed in the blue sky over the island as the German airborne assault began. The garrison, ill-provided and exhausted by the Grecian campaign, was overrun by the highly trained and well-armed German force. Once more the British army had to be evacuated and of 28,000 men engaged only half escaped to Egypt.

After the attempt by the British Eighth Army to relieve Tobruk by 'Operation Battle-Axe' had fizzled out in a stalemate, General Auchinleck, who had replaced Wavell, began to build up for a decisive battle in the desert. Before he could take the offensive, however, Rommel seized the initiative. After a fortnight's fierce fighting, the German armoured divisions captured a commanding ridge at Knightsbridge and, as the British fell back, Rommel turned the full force of the attack against the isolated garrison of Tobruk. Within four days the fortress had fallen, its 25,000 defenders were made prisoner and vast quantities of material were captured. Before the British could reform, Rommel again attacked. Only shortage of German supplies and a hastily constructed British defence position at El Alamein halted his advance about sixty miles short of Alexandria.

The bewildering swiftness of the German victory, the capture of Tobruk and the new threat to the Suez Canal was a staggering blow, the position threatening to bring about the loss of the Middle East and the road to India.

The situation of the Mediterranean fleet was now unenviable. They were facing a more powerful and more modern fleet, which had many alternative bases from which to operate. German and Italian bombers could dominate most of the Western Mediterranean from airfields in Sicily and Sardinia; and, with practically the whole of the north-eastern shores of Africa, and with Crete and Greece in its hands, the Axis was astride the Eastern Mediterranean as well. As Rommel's threat to Alexandria made this important British naval base insecure, steps were taken immediately after the defeat in the desert to evacuate all capital ships, leaving only a cruiser squadron and a few destroyers and minesweepers.

The British fleet at Gibraltar was already seriously reduced in strength by the demands of the Far East and it was almost suicidally dangerous to send a fleet into the Western Mediterranean at all. Yet it was vitally necessary to keep this sea route open; for almost midway between Gibraltar and Alexandria, and surrounded on all sides by the enemy, stood Malta, the one unconquered British bastion in the inner Mediterranean.

In the midst of so many disastrous losses, the reduction of this island fortress might have seemed relatively unimportant, but naval strategists believed it to be the key to the Mediterranean strategy. Admiral Sir Andrew Cunningham, following the title of Churchill's book on this troubled period of the war, called it 'The Linchpin of the Hinge of Fate', and so it was to prove. It can now be seen that the fate of the Middle East and India and the whole Allied cause depended on its successful defence.

At this crucial period of the war – in August 1942, when the British had reached the nadir of their hopes – the Island was almost lost. Bombed, starved and apparently without hope of further supply, its defenders were reaching the point of capitulation.

II

More than 150 years ago, Nelson wrote: 'I now declare that I consider Malta as a most important outwork of India, that will ever give us great influence in the Levant, and indeed all the southern parts of Italy. In this view, I hope we shall never give it up.'

This was perhaps the first realization of the Island's importance in the modern conception of global war, but as long as man has sailed the blue waters of the Mediterranean, warring races have fought for its possession, because of its wonderful harbour and because of its commanding position at the crossroads of a sea whose shores saw the dawn of Western civilization.

Through recorded history each dominant Mediterranean people held it as an entrepot of trade in peace and a citadel in war from which the approaches to three continents could be commanded. In turn it was occupied by Phœnicians, Greeks and Carthaginians. In Roman times it became a stronghold of *mare nostrum* for maintaining the peace of the Empire and with the Roman decline it passed to the land-hungry Normans, next to the Moors and then to the Spanish. Charles the Fifth of Spain gave it to the Knights of St John, and this austere and warlike order of chivalry defended Malta for Christendom for more than 200 years. Then Napoleon took it from them on his way to Egypt.

The people of Malta, however, resented French rule and rebelled so successfully that, with the help of Nelson, they won back their Island. At their own request, they became part of the British Empire.

Thus, Malta has been a British naval base since the early nineteenth century, but did not prove to be of decisive importance until the rise of the dictatorships in the late thirties. As the warlike intentions of Hitler and Mussolini became plain, grave fears began to be felt at the British Admiralty for the safety of the Island. The army and the air force were less preoccupied with holding Malta in event of a war against the Axis, for at that time no one had envisaged the fall of France and the consequent importance the Island was to assume as an air staging point on the route to the East, once French aerodromes were denied to Britain.

Moreover, many strategists considered that, with the rise of air-power, the Island, lying within sixty miles of the Sicilian airfields, would be untenable in the event of Italy's entry into the war.

Some authorities consider that its defence was the turning point of the whole war and the crux of Hitler's overall strategic defeat. F. M. Hinsley, in his book, *Hitler's Strategy* emphasizes the importance of Malta to final British success in the desert and considers that it was by failing to capture it that Hitler lost the war strategically.

Rommel, writing retrospectively (*Rommel Papers* edited by B. H. Liddell Hart) believed: 'With Malta in our hands, the British would have had little chance of exercising any further control over convoy traffic in the Central Mediterranean . . . it has the lives of many thousands of German and Italian soldiers on its conscience.'

His chief of staff, General Fritz Bayerlein wrote in *Fatal Decisions*: '. . . until the air and naval base at Malta ceased to act as a constant thorn in the flesh of our rearward communications, there was no possibility of the situation at the front improving and therefore no prospect of capturing the Nile Delta.'

Finally, Churchill in *The Second World War*: 'The interrelation between Malta and the desert operations was never so plain as in 1942, and the heroic defence of the Island in that year formed the keystone of the prolonged struggle for the maintenance of our position in Egypt and the Middle East.'

At the beginning of the war, however, with the possible exception of Churchill, only the British naval command considered Malta to be vital to Middle Eastern strategy.

On the German side there was one man who also understood the significance of the Island and he too was a sailor. From the start, Grand Admiral Raeder had emphasized the importance of Malta at the Nazi war councils. Fortunately for the free world, this far-seeing man seldom had the ear of Hitler, who distrusted all his naval advisers.

When the admiral visited the Führer's headquarters in Berlin on 13 February 1942, however, he found a gratified Hitler ready to listen to his plans, for the three German cruisers had just run the gauntlet of the English Channel successfully and the German Navy was for once in firm favour with the Nazi leader.

While Hitler revelled in the discomfort which this would be causing his enemies, Raeder considered the scheme he meant to lay before him, now that he was in such a rare receptive mood. It was a plan immense in its potentialities. It envisaged not only the conquest of the Middle East, but the overthrow of India and the junction between the Italo-German and Japanese forces.

Raeder sketched out the strategic background of his vision which was to be accomplished by a giant pincer movement. The German armies, when they had beaten Russia, were to swing to the right through the Caucasus and into the Middle East. Meanwhile, Rommel, after beating the British in Egypt, would take the Suez Canal and sweep up through Syria to join them. Then, united, the Germans with the Italian allies would drive through Persia into India. With the Japanese co-ordinating their attack from the East, India, already seething with political unrest, would be impossible to defend, and the Axis would build a wall of armour from Berlin to Tokyo.

Apart from tactical gains, the success of such a movement would entail the virtual collapse of the British

Empire. It would also relieve once and for all the chronic shortage of oil which was then a serious threat to the Axis war machine, for both the Caucasian and Middle Eastern oil fields would be overrun and denied to the Allies. Also, in the early stages of this huge pincer movement each of the two thrusts would be of complementary value to the other, because if the German armies succeeded in breaking through in one theatre only, they would outflank the defenders in the other theatre and hasten defeat there too.

Raeder maintained, and Hitler this time agreed, that victory in the Mediterranean theatre and to some extent in the Russian theatre as well, depended on two factors: sea power and the co-operation between naval, land and air forces. The object of Mediterranean strategy would be to co-ordinate the whole movement, with sea power ensuring supplies, supplies ensuring bases and bases ensuring sea power. It would be necessary first of all to eliminate the constant threat of British naval and air forces striking from Malta against their supply route. The capture of Malta would be the first step towards the capture of Egypt, Persia and, ultimately India. It would also constitute an important base for the operations.

Hitler was fired by this vision. On the practical side, he saw that it fitted into the operations then in train in Russia and North Africa. He immediately ordered that all long-range strategic considerations were to be subordinated to the plan – the 'Great Plan' as he himself christened it.

III

Two major strategic events had immediately preceded the conception of the 'Great Plan'.

In the first place, the drive deeper into Russia had been frozen into immobility by winter, thereby releasing a large part of the Luftwaffe for other duties. In the second, the strength of the Afrika Korps had been dangerously sapped by the sea and air offensive from Malta, to such an extent that if the German attack in the desert was to continue, a counter-offensive had to be mounted against the Island.

The German reactions were a sustained air attack on Malta and then, as a prelude to the implementation of the 'Great Plan', combined Italo-German preparations for the capture of the Island called 'Operation Hercules'.

Half-hearted moves towards the latter end had already been made by the Italians. Indeed it is surprising that they had not made greater efforts, because the Italian High Command had decided, as a result of fleet manœuvres as early as 1938, that Malta could be taken without difficulty. When Italy entered the war, lack of military preparedness on the Island would have made such an operation easy, for the defences consisted only of 172 AA guns. There was a complete absence of fighter defence. Moreover, there were no reserves of food, and a determined blockade could have starved out the population within a matter of weeks.

Realizing their nakedness, Admiral Ford, the senior naval officer on Malta, searched the stores and found the crated parts of four old Gladiator biplanes in a warehouse and immediately had them assembled. One was irreparably damaged in the first Italian air-raid of the war, but the remaining three wrote themselves a veritable saga in the skies over the beleaguered Island. Manned by volunteers from the staff of Air Commodore F. A. M. Maynard, the air officer commanding, and christened by the Maltese *Faith, Hope* and *Charity*, they took off day after day against the Italian air armadas. Though obsolete, they did considerable execution against a vastly superior enemy, forced the Italians to provide fighter escorts and served as an invaluable morale-booster to the defenders until the slow build-up of fighter defence on the Island could begin.

On the direct orders from Churchill, Hurricanes earmarked for home defence were flown out to Malta in successive 'penny packets' until local air superiority was attained, making it possible for submarines, cruisers and bomber squadrons to follow. The attack on the Axis trans-Mediterranean supply route to North Africa then began in earnest and the sharpened sword of Malta cut deep. Like the corsairs of old, British sailors and airmen swept out from the Island by day and by night making scattered flotsam of the heavily-laden troop ships, tankers and merchantmen. In June 1941 alone, seventy-three per cent of the German-controlled shipping from Italy was sunk and this figure had risen to seventy-seven per cent by November.

Hitler had long been warned that this unhappy situation would result from neglecting the significance of Malta, but the warning had fallen on deaf ears. At that time all his febrile energies were devoted to the projected attack on Russia to an extent that he even told Admiral Raeder that 'the loss of North Africa could be withstood from a military point of view'. The slowing down of the Russian campaign, however, coupled with appeals from Rommel and the Italian High Command, made him change his mind and in October 1941, he announced that he intended 'to transfer the centre of military operations to the Mediterranean'. He then gave orders for the movement of a complete air group, Luftflotte II, which had been responsible for air operations before Moscow, to Southern Italy. Generalfeldmarschall Kesselring was sent to take command of this and Luftflotte X which was already stationed in Sicily. These formations, together with the Italian Air Force, gave Kesselring, as Commander-in-Chief Air South, the control of 2,000 first-line aircraft. His mission was defined by Hiter as, among other things, to 'gain control of the air and sea between South Italy and North Africa and thus ensure safe lines of communication with Libya and

Cyrenaica: in this connection the neutralization of Malta is especially important . . .'

The Axis air attack fell on Malta with crushing violence. Despite fierce resistance offered by the defenders, airfields were blasted, the harbour laid in ruins and the scale of the offensive against Axis shipping, and even the Island's ability to defend itself, fast diminished. By February 1942, Kesselring was able to report to Goering that Axis shipping losses had been reduced from between seventy and eighty per cent to less than thirty per cent. Supplies began to flow again into Libya enabling the Afrika Korps to build up for its final thrust towards the Suez Canal.

While the air attack proceeded, Hitler, convinced of the practicability of the 'Great Plan', gave in to the united pleas of Axis commanders on the spot and agreed to mount 'Operation Hercules' as a combined Italo-German attack on Malta. Final top-level arrangements were made at a meeting between the two dictators at Berchtesgaden on 29 April 1942. The Italians, represented by Mussolini, Count Ciano and the Italian Commander-in-Chief, Marshal Cavallero, were greeted at Puhl station with great cordiality by Hiter, Ribbentrop and Jodl and housed in Klessheim Castle, which was resplendent with antique furniture, hangings and carpets looted from occupied France. At the conference, Hitler harangued his listeners with long and optimistic reviews of the war, one of which lasted an hour and forty minutes. Mussolini took surreptitious glances at his wrist-watch and Jodl fell asleep. Finally, on the second day, the two parties got down to business. The date for the assault was fixed for early June and, on the German side, Hitler agreed to send two paratroop battalions, an engineer battalion and an unspecified number of German naval barges. On the Italian side, Mussolini agreed to supply the parachute divisions of two regiments, a battalion of engineers and five batteries, besides sea transports and a heavy naval escort.

The Duce also reported that for five months, 10,000 Italian commandos had been exercising on the coast of Livorno, which is similar in formation to the south-east coast of Malta, using specially constructed scaling ladders by means of which they hoped to mount the 120-feet-high cliffs from their landing craft.

Broadly, the campaign plan envisaged seizure of the south-eastern edge of Malta by airborne troops as a jumping-off base for an assault on the airfields south of the town and harbour of Valletta, after a bomber blitz had softened up the defences. The main attack by naval forces and landing parties was to be mounted against strong points south of Valletta in conjunction with another paratroop attack on the harbour itself and further bombing of the coastal batteries. A diversionary attack from the sea was also to be made against the bay of Marsa Scirocco.

With these broad details settled, the conference broke up with mutual expressions of regard, and the Italian party returned home.

Training now proceeded with great energy and there seemed every chance that the operation would be successful. The forces allocated were adequate and none of the German commanders, except perhaps Goering and Hitler himself, seem to have had any misgivings about a swift victory, despite their reluctance to trust the Italians in any major venture.

There then supervened one of those strange strategic counter-marches, sudden vacillations and moments of doubt which underlie so many momentous decisions of war.

On the Italian side a defeatist attitude was evident before the Berchtesgaden meeting. Count Ciano recorded in his diary that on the eve of the meeting, Cavallero realized that the capture of Malta was a 'tough nut'. In May, Ciano again wrote: 'Colonel Cassero (one of the operational commanders) does not share Cavallero's enthusiasm for the attack on Malta ... Even Fourier

(Italian Secretary for Air) is anxious about a landing operation . . .' Again in June: 'There is . . . some hesitation about the Malta undertaking . . .' and 'I am more than ever of the opinion that the undertaking will never take place.'

General Carboni, who commanded an assault division, was pessimistic from the start and anticipated 'a general drowning'. This son of an American mother appears to have intrigued in Italian court circles against the mounting of 'Hercules', for he boasted openly later that it was a letter which he had had conveyed to the Prince of Piedmont, heir to the Italian throne, which finally prejudiced the High Command against the assault.

Despite the Italian uneasiness, a word from Hitler could have launched the parachute regiments, ships and assault craft against the beleaguered island, but he hesitated. It was essentially a seaborne operation, and throughout the war, he seemed unable to come to firm decisions when planning naval action. In a confiding moment, he once admitted to Raeder: 'I am a hero on land and a coward at sea.'

There is, however, no doubt that any reluctance on his part must have been reinforced by his advisers as well as by the increasing coolness of the Italians themselves towards the project. According to the Italians, Rommel was entirely to blame for the Führer's change of heart and this view is also accepted by Churchill. Kesselring in his memoirs declares flatly: 'Hitler and the German High Command must share with the Commando Supremo the blame for that wrong decision. They were admittedly less able to appreciate the situation correctly once Rommel had got his propaganda machine working properly . . . At that period Rommel exercised an almost hypnotic influence over Hitler, who was all but incapable of appreciating the situation objectively.'

One undisputed fact is that there were insufficient troops and air forces to mount simultaneously both the attack on Malta and Rommel's drive towards the Suez Canal and the Middle East. Rommel's critics say that in

—

the elation of capturing Tobruk he imagined he would have sufficient supplies to drive straight through to Alexandria without waiting for Malta to be liquidated, and advised Hitler accordingly. That he had frequently argued for the capture of Malta is, however, attested both by his staff and by many of his dispatches, but in a radio message to the German High Command on 22 June 1942, he requested that Mussolini be prevailed upon to remove Italian restrictions on the movement of his troops pending 'Operation Hercules'.

On the 24th, a note from Hitler was handed to Mussolini which began: 'Fate, Duce, has presented us with an opportunity which will not occur a second time,' and asked him to support the continuance of the thrust towards Alexandria, as both Rommel and the Italian commander believed that they could annihilate the British troops with the forces at their command. On the 24th, the Commando Supremo officially postponed the attack on Malta, and on the 30th Mussolini complied with the Führer's request.

Whatever 'hypnotic influence' Rommel may have exerted over his leader in this fateful choice it seems reasonable to assume that Hitler's own reluctance towards the venture may have played some part. He may also have been powerfully influenced by Kesselring's own glowing account of the results achieved by the bombing of Malta, for this indicated that the Island was no longer in a condition to interfere effectively in the designs of the Axis.

Indeed the bombing of Malta had had considerable effect and there is no doubt that this and the Axis air control over the sea routes had all but succeeded in their purpose.

In August 1942, the Island, though still fighting back, was within less than a month of starvation. The defenders were in a desperate plight and it seemed impossible for the British to fight a convoy through the Mediterranean to relieve them.

CHAPTER TWO

Hold Fast and We Win

In an underground office of the Residency, Sir Edward Jackson, Deputy Governor of Malta, was drafting a report on the situation.

The sounds of battle filtered down from above, diminished by the solid rock from which the cellar was hewn and the blast walls which protected it from the ground level, but the scream of straining aero engines and the regular crump of bombs could plainly be heard.

The Deputy Governor hardly stirred, however, even when a near explosion shook the table at which he was writing, and precipitated a dusty rain of tiny rock particles on the white paper before him. Months of such experiences had hardened him, as it had hardened most of the civil and military population of Malta, to the fury of enemy air attack.

'. . . just received information from the Secretary of State for the Colonies that it has been decided that it is impracticable in present conditions to send a direct convoy to Malta from the west . . .' he wrote. '. . . the situation of the civil population is the same as that of any other section of the fortress in that it can hold out if sufficient supplies are received, and cannot if they are not. If the civil population collapses, the whole fortress collapses . . .'

This was Sir Edward's main preoccupation. On the Governor's Council he represented the interests of the civil population, and he had also the unenviable task of announcing to the civil population the progressive cuts in their rations, and of explaining their necessity.

He paused in his writing, and his mind wandered back into history. This was a commonplace of warfare, that

the strength of a fortress depended on the health and
morale of the civil population. Strong walls were
powerless to protect if the will within was sapped by
starvation. It was obvious, and yet how different to be
experiencing the diminishing supplies of a beleaguered
garrison rather than reading in a history book 'the
defenders were starving and the castle fell'.

He took up his pen again: 'I say that for the following
reasons,' he wrote.

'(a) It is impossible to secure essential services from
or even to maintain order among 270,000 people if they
are not fed.

'(b) It is impracticable to quell the civil population by
the use of military force, firstly because one-third of the
garrison consists of Maltese troops whose families
would be subjected to that force and secondly because
probably opinion in England would react violently to
the application of military force for such reasons to a
population of whom they have come to think as they
now think of the Maltese . . .'

Yes, it was difficult for people in Britain to realize the
desperate predicament they were in on this little island.

'The question, therefore, arises, how long can the civil
population hold out . . .'

The situation about which Sir Edward was writing
and had been writing for some months in the same
strain had resulted from another measure of neglect in
peacetime which could not be rectified once the
demands of war had swallowed up available material.

Guns and fighters which could have ensured the
Island's supply route had not been sent in peacetime and
now in war they were desperately needed elsewhere.

On this rocky mass of limestone, slightly less than
116 square miles in extent, smaller than the Isle of
Wight, and the most densely populated area in Europe,
the result of this neglect was more serious than on any
other British possession. From the outbreak of war with
Italy, the civil population of more than a quarter of a

million, augmented by 180,000 troops, had been short of
food.

In the past, with far smaller populations, Malta had
never been self-supporting, and the agricultural trends
of the past hundred years had aggravated the situation.
In 1918, for instance, the Island had grown about 20,000
acres of wheat. In 1942, after strenuous efforts to return
to full productivity, only 12,000 acres were cropped.

The cause of this was mainly economic. The people
had drifted away from cereal production between the
wars to plant vineyards. Corn could then be bought
cheaply from Italy and there was always a good sale for
wine. So the Island's ability to support itself had further
declined. Sicily, being the nearest land, had provided
much of her imports, and on the outbreak of war these
had been suddenly cut off.

Moreover, the Maltese are largely a *pasta*-eating
people to whom spaghetti, macaroni and bread are
unvariable necessities of life; so corn, bulky and difficult
to ship, had somehow to be brought to the Island.

When the emergency arrived, the Royal Navy and
Mercantile Marine stepped into the breach and convoys
retained the level of Malta's supplies with varying success through 1940 and 1941. Food was rationed and
often short, but no great hardship was experienced.
Though difficult, the position had not become alarming.

Even at the beginning of the Kesselring blitz, one
convoy of three merchant vessels got through early in
January, losing only the ammunition ship *Thermopylae*.
Such a situation was, however, too good to last. The year
of 1942 opened with an ominous event for the safety of
Malta: the fall of Benghazi on the 25th of January. The
airfields of Cyrenaica, which, until then had been giving
fighter protection to the ships bringing food to the defenders of Malta, now harboured German bombers menacing both the Island and its best supply route.

The Axis net was closing and the enemy surrounding
Malta on all sides.

—

Evidence of the new danger was not long in coming, for the next convoy met with disaster.

On the 12th of February, the merchantmen *Clan Chattan, Clan Campbell* and *Rowallan Castle* sailed from Alexandria, escorted at first by the anti-aircraft cruiser *Carlisle* and eight destroyers. Some hours later Admiral Vian followed with two cruisers of the 15th Squadron and eight more destroyers.

On the following day *Clan Campbell* was narrowly missed by a stick of bombs and so severely damaged that she had to limp in to Tobruk. On the 14th *Clan Chattan* received a direct hit and caught fire, and the same afternoon *Rowallan Castle* was disabled. Both these ships had to be sunk by our own forces and, therefore, no supplies reached Malta.

This precipitated an immediate crisis in the Island. Admiral Cunningham had already reported, on the 7th of February, that Malta had petrol sufficient to last only until the 1st of August, and that fuel oil and other essential material would scarcely be sufficient to last until the end of May.

It was also true that for the bombers and torpedo aircraft to range far out into the Mediterranean severing the life-line of Rommel's Panzer army from Italy, petrol had to be brought to their aerodromes, and, indeed, their offensive was one of the chief reasons for holding Malta at all; but it was the shortage of wheat and flour for bread which caused Sir Edward the greatest anxiety. The ability of the RAF and the Fleet Air Arm to continue their offensive depended on the health and survival of the air crews, the men servicing the planes, repairing the air strips and manning the guns, and on the islanders who backed them.

Great though the contribution of the Air Arm was to both the offensive and defensive power of the Island, it was of a purely military nature. Moreover, the fighter defence was local in effect, and extended its protection only to a small part of the voyage and any convoy attempting to reach the Grand Harbour.

As Sir Edward Jackson and other leaders on the Island realized, therefore, Malta stood or fell by the condition of the civil population and fuel oil and kerosene were as much basic needs for civilian well-being as flour.

Wood was a rare and valuable commodity. Moreover, coal, the most bulky of all fuel sources, was expensive and difficult to transport. As a result, the traditional dependence of the Maltese on kerosene for lighting, heating and cooking had been increased beyond measure by wartime conditions.

The power for nearly all public utilities was supplied by oil-burning units. The bakeries, electric power for hospitals and essential industries, the water supply and sewage works all depended ultimately on oil. Without it the whole complex of community life in the Island would have broken down.

Without oil, too, the chances of a convoy arriving at Malta at all were greatly diminished. Before any ships could enter the Grand Harbour, island-based sweepers had to clear the channel and approaches of mines which were replaced nightly by Axis aircraft, submarines and E-boats. These sweepers were mainly oil-burning ships. Then there was the necessity to refuel lighter escort units and merchantmen for the return journey to Gibraltar. The very cranes which aided the speedy unloading of goods – and the convoy now about to be described proved how vital such speed could be – derived their motive power from oil.

So it was, that as the Axis blockade tightened on Malta, oil and kerosene became, with bread, the materials upon which the fate of the Island basically rested.

The overwhelming of the February convoy and the desperate shortages which now threatened the beleaguered fortress alarmed the War Cabinet, and a decision was immediately taken to sail another convoy at the earliest possible date.

It consisted of the naval supply ship *Breconshire*,

carrying a large quantity of fuel oil, and the merchantmen *Clan Campbell, Pampas* and *Talabot.*

These ships sailed from Alexandria on the 20th of
March and unluckily this coincided with the launching
of the all-out bombing offensive against Malta by the
German forces in Sicily and Sardinia.

Admiral Vian's escort was one of the heaviest thus far
committed, four cruisers and sixteen destroyers, while
another cruiser and a flotilla leader sailed from Malta to
join them.

Enemy air reconnaissance soon reported the convoy,
and within twelve hours Admiral Vian knew that a
major sea battle was imminent, for the British submarine P.36 signalled early on the 21st that heavy units of
the Italian Navy were leaving Taranto.

These were the battleship *Littorio,* mounting nine 15-
inch guns, *Gorizia* and *Trento,* cruisers with 8-inch
armament, and the 6-inch gun cruiser *Giovanni Delle
Bande Nere,* with ten escorting destroyers.

Despite the fact that he was heavily out-gunned, for
only one of his cruisers mounted calibres as heavy as 6-
inch, the admiral was in no doubt about engaging the
enemy. The convoy sailed on towards Malta and the
cruisers steamed to intercept the Italian fleet.

The second Battle of Sirte which followed remains the
finest example of protective cruiser action. Again and
again, the British ships, dodging in and out of smoke
screens, turned the greatly superior enemy force away
from the merchantmen. Though fourteen destroyers
were damaged, the Italian fleet finally retired without
accomplishing the destruction of the convoy and the
British fleet set out to return to Alexandria in a rising
gale.

In the meantime, however, the merchantmen, delayed
by the battle, had to complete the final dash to Malta
dispersed and in daylight, with a meagre escort, all ships
of which were short of AA ammunition.

Only twenty miles from Malta, *Clan Campbell* was

sighted by German bombers and sank quickly following
a number of direct hits.

Breconshire, with her precious cargo of oil, got to
within eight miles of the Island before she too was hit
and disabled. High seas prevented the cruiser *Penelope*
from towing her to the Grand Harbour and she had to be
beached at Marsaxlokk. She was sunk there two days
later by German bombers with only a fraction of her oil
cargo salved.

Though *Pampas* and *Talabot* sailed into the harbour
and the population lined the battlements to cheer them
in, under 6,000 tons of their combined cargo of 26,000
tons of foodstuffs and ammunition had been unloaded
when both were sunk at their moorings by German dive-
bombers.

So, despite the winning of a great naval victory, the
purpose of the convoy had not been achieved.

Apart from small quantities of supplies brought in by
submarines, by the fast mine-layers *Welshman* and
Manxman, and the pittance salved from the March
convoy, Malta had received no supplies since January.

On the 1st of April, General Dobbie, the Governor,
signalled the War Office: 'Our supply position has been
reassessed and may be summarized as follows:

(a) Wheat and flour. No material cuts seem possible,
as these are staple foods. Present stocks will, with
care, last until early June.

(b) Fodder. Issues already inadequate were recently
cut; stocks will now last until end of June.

(c) Minor foodstuffs. Meat stocks are entirely
exhausted. Most other stocks will last until June.

(d) White oils. Aviation fuel till mid-August; benzine
till mid-June; kerosene till early July.

(e) Black oils. We have only 920 tons of diesel oil (five
weeks' supply) and 2,000 tons of furnace fuel, all of
which will be needed for fuelling HM ships now in

—

dock. The black oil position is thus becoming precarious, and very urgent action appears necessary to restore it.

(f) Coal. Welsh coal will last only until end of May ... other grades until mid-June.

(g) Ammunition. Consumption of ack-ack ammunition has greatly increased ... and we have only one and a half months' stock left ...'

By 15 April 1942, when the King's award of the George Cross to the Island was announced, its plight was thus desperate.

'It is obvious that the very worst must happen if we cannot replenish our vital needs ...' General Dobbie informed the home Government.

Two months later, when the new Governor, Viscount Gort, presented the medal at a special investiture ceremony, starvation and consequent surrender were only a matter of days away.

For civilians, rations had declined until the bread issue stood at only ten and a half ounces a day and flour and rice were unobtainable. In Britain, during the whole of the war, it was never necessary to ration bread and flour. It must also be remembered that bread and flour were the staple Maltese diet, so that the half a pound a week British meat ration, tinned meats, baked beans and other rationed goods to be had in the United Kingdom must be included with bread and flour to gain a proper comparison.

Most Maltese dishes during happier times included olive oil; but stocks had now been completely consumed and the fat ration of lard and margarine (with the very occasional substitute of butter) amounted only to three and a half ounces a week, a little more than a third of the British issue.

Milk which was unrationed in England, where tinned milk could also be had, was unobtainable in Malta, and a strictly limited amount of powdered milk was doled

out to invalids, infants under seven years of age and
expectant mothers only. Cheese in the United Kingdom
was issued at the rate of four ounces a week per person
– in Malta only one and three-quarters of an ounce was
available.

The Maltese were accustomed to drinking as much
coffee as the English drink tea, and the restriction of the
coffee issue to one and three-quarters of an ounce a
week between three people was perhaps the greatest
hardship of all, far greater than that represented by the
allowance of two ounces of tea issued to each person in
England.

Most other necessities were unobtainable. There was
no sugar ration, and jam and sweets had long been things
remembered from the past. The British ration allowed
six ounces of sugar and a pound of jam a week. Potatoes
and vegetables were also in fair supply in Britain, but,
apart from an occasional issue of about one pound a
head of potatoes, the average Maltese went without; the
restricted amounts of vegetables produced locally, usually too small to justify workable rationing, disappeared
on to the black market where they commanded very
high prices.

Apart from one hot meal issued each day in Victory
Kitchens, which began to be set up all over the Island at
the end of this period, the Maltese had no means of
augmenting this meagre supply of food except on the
black market, which, as in every other country during
wartime, flourished despite all efforts to counter it by
the authorities. Prices prevailing for unauthorized supplies were, however, well beyond the pocket of more
than ninety per cent of the Maltese. A pound of sugar
cost a pound for instance. Apart from minute quantities
of goats' meat issued to the Victory Kitchens in July and
August 1942, there had been no legitimate meat supplies
for a year, and a pound of beef, when it could be had at
the risk of a heavy fine, cost over a pound. Chickens
fetched between one pound fifteen shillings and five

pounds, and rabbits sold easily at twenty shillings. Small quantities of fish could be obtained for about five shillings a pound, and eggs at one time reached three and six each.

Yet these reliefs from a bare diet were only for the few, and the level of rationing to which the vast majority were tied, was well below the level necessary to maintain health, particularly as it came after six months of food restrictions. And it could be reduced no further. Troops' rations had similarly been reduced to the barest minimum.

Quite apart from food, the situation was grim in the extreme. Most of those things considered as ordinary requirements of civilized life were lacking, and most of the unnecessary but sought-after amenities which contribute much to the morale of people facing difficult times had gone.

The tobacco shortage was most distressing to a large proportion of the population. Two days of the week were fixed for the issue of one packet of cigarettes or tobacco to each man between sixteen and sixty.

It was a commonplace feature of Maltese life to see up to a hundred or more people sleeping out the night on the pavement outside the tobacco shops when an issue was due the following morning. Pipe smokers soon took to a mixture of dried fig, lemon and strawberry leaves which that 'mother of invention' discovered to be the best herbal substitute for tobacco.

Cinemas, owing to the shortage of oil for electric power, were rigidly curtailed, although these shows were considered important morale-boosters. When shows were given, patrons had to find their way to their seats in a pitch-dark auditorium without house lights.

All sorts of alcoholic drinks also began to disappear as soon as the Axis blockade tightened. Most of the breweries had converted to oil-burning machinery, owing to the early shortage of coal, and then had to shut down altogether because of the shortage of oil. So there was no beer.

With the disappearance of beer the run on spirits soon exhausted all stocks except those of rum. As in most purely naval ports and establishments, quantities of rum could always be found, but the demand soon forced this out of general circulation and on to the black market where it sold at 200 per cent above the controlled price.

Most of the ordinary commodities of everyday life were now absent or in very short supply.

The women had had to give up using cosmetics because they were unobtainable even on the black market. Similarly, brushes and combs and even shoe polish could not be bought for any amount of money. Soap was rationed to about half a pound a person once a fortnight.

New clothes were a luxury few could afford, a good suit or stylish dress fetching nearly ten times their pre-war prices. It was now a question of mend and make do, with cotton at ten shillings a reel. Old clothes were patched and patched again until they held together no longer. All pretensions to smartness had gone, and indeed good clothes came to be regarded as a badge of social unworthiness and the brand of the black market racketeer. In the prevailing climate, this was less of a hardship than it would have been in higher latitudes, but the acute shortage of shoe leather on this rocky island was serious. New shoes and sandals could only be obtained at prohibitive prices; and so, as old ones wore out, they were replaced by home-made clogs of boxwood with canvas uppers. These were usually uncomfortable and often hurt the feet intolerably.

For many years, in most parts of Malta, water had been accepted as an integral part of life, as in other civilized urban areas. A limitless supply, it seemed, could always be obtained simply by turning on a tap. That too was changed, and water was rationed to nine gallons a day for each person: less than one-third of the average British wartime consumption. With the hot, sticky Mediterranean climate in which regular baths and showers alone can make life comfortable, this was also a great hardship.

For the housewife especially, the situation had become dull, difficult and dangerous. Denied make-up, pretty clothes and most of her spare-time amusements, cooking became a burden and she often had to forage for her fuel like a primitive savage. The allotment of a quarter of a gallon of kerosene a week to each family of two, was insufficient to supply proper heating and lighting, and so camp-fire cooking could be found throughout Malta. In the country the garden became the kitchen. In the town, where few homes have gardens, it was in the street outside the front door. Open fireplaces were carved out of stone or improvised from oil drums. The women paid their daily call to the nearest bomb-ruined buildings and returned with wood and kindling to cook the dinner. Washing up was a nightmare, for the wood smoke sooted up their pots and pans, and the lack of artificial cleaners had to be made up for with sand and elbow grease. If a piece of crockery was smashed it could not be replaced, and already many families drank their meagre coffee ration out of rough-rimmed glasses made from cutting off the bottoms of bottles.

These privations would have been bad enough without the continual threat of destruction and death and the wail of sirens heralding the approach of terror. It is now a well-attested principle of wartime psychology that bombing for a time stiffens the morale and brings out a hidden fortitude and toughness in most people; but for the women of Malta, faced with appalling difficulties in everyday life, it was becoming too heavy a trial. The constant danger to their children, to their men, many of them working in the most heavily-bombed target areas, to their homes and to everyone and everything they held dear, was slowly sapping their resistance. Nor was this surprising. The wonder of it was that they had not given in weeks before, for the Island was fast being reduced to rubble by German and Italian bombers.

By the end of May 1942, Malta had suffered 2,470 air-raids and between the 1st of January and the 24th of July there was only one raidless period of twenty-four hours. Those who remember the blitz on London in 1940 and the interminable succession of days on days when the sirens sounded and the bombs came raining down will understand just what that meant. Yet the longest number of consecutive days on which London was raided amounted to only 57, while the Maltese had suffered no less than 154 days of continual day and night bombing. The total tonnage of bombs dropped on the Island during March and April alone was twice that dropped in London during the year of its worst attacks, and, in one month, 6,000 tons of high explosive had rocked the Island's towns and villages.

Loss of civilian lives had been heavy enough to shake the fortitude of a lesser people. From the outbreak of war until December 1941, 330 had been killed and 297 seriously injured. With the coming of the Luftwaffe, the next 4 months was a period of death and disaster, for 820 people were killed and 915 seriously injured. Another 158 were killed and 383 injured in the following 3 months.

Had it not been for the nature of the rock upon which Malta is founded a far higher proportion of the population might have been wiped out and essential civil and military services completely disrupted. The natural process of erosion had formed hundreds of natural caverns below the shallow topsoil. Moreover, the construction of man-made rock shelters was made easier by the fact that the limestone is easily cut into but soon weathers to an iron-hard consistency on exposure to air.

As a result, ample underground accommodation had been constructed before the war to house oil-storage

tanks, generators and workshops and to shelter a large
proportion of the population during air-raids. Most of
this work was inspired by Admiral Sir W. T. R. Ford, the
Senior British Naval Officer, who plainly foresaw the
trial by fire through which the Island was to pass. He
also had thousands of picks made in the naval workshops, and with these the Maltese had been able to
construct their own shelters.

Though these early precautions saved thousands of
Maltese lives, no means could be found to protect their
homes. As a result, 10,000 houses lay in ruins, 20,000
others had sustained serious damage and nearly 100
churches had been gutted.

For days on end, roads remained blocked with debris
and were impassable, for neither the manpower nor the
petrol was available to clear them.

In the bigger towns like Valletta, Senglea, Cospicua
and Vittoriosa, the limited water supply suffered frequent breakdowns, some lasting for several days. The
sanitary services were often interrupted for as much as
a week and the telephone was more often cut off than in
use.

Frequently, even the almost superhuman efforts of the
Malta Water Department failed for long periods to cope
with the demands of emergency fresh-water lines. Then
the mobile water bowsers had to be sent out and at each
stop fifty or more men, women and children would
queue up with every pot, pan or ewer available, for they
knew from experience that the petrol shortage would
prevent another visit perhaps for many days.

A depressing desolation was everywhere to be found.
No town or village was untouched, and wherever the
eye rested dust and rubble disfigured the view. That dust
had become a curse. In many places one waded through
it ankle deep, and when the wind blew strongly it
became a dirty yellow sandstorm which penetrated the
cracks in the windows and swirled in under the doors. It
grated on the teeth, got in the eyes and spoiled the food.

'If the civil population collapses, the whole fortress collapses . . .' Sir Edward Jackson wrote.

At every scarred street corner, behind the bar in every pub or club, spread over the still-warm ruins of homes, shops and churches, could be found gigantic pictures of Churchill with that bulldog slogan: 'Hold Fast and We Win'.

Through every sort of privation, difficulty and danger, through fire, ruin and death, the Maltese had held fast when none could have blamed them for loosening their hold.

Now, however, the hour approached when little more could be expected of flesh and blood. Already the long period of pitifully deficient diet had begun to manifest itself in skin and enteric diseases associated with malnutrition. Soon there would be nothing at all to eat, nothing to turn the wheels of this tiny island society. Then the white flag would fly above Malta.

CHAPTER THREE

Target Date 'Surrender'

I

A secret date for Malta's capitulation had been calculated from month to month by General Dobbie, the Governor, and after him by Lord Gort, and by a committee consisting of the Deputy Governor, Sir Edward Jackson and the chiefs of the three services.

This involved no complicated evaluation of circumstances; it depended simply on how long vital stocks of flour, fuel oil, kerosene and, to a lesser extent, petrol and anti-aircraft ammunition would last.

When these were exhausted the Island and all upon it would have to surrender.

The question of evacuating the Island, even by the troops defending it, never arose as a practical proposition because the means to do so did not exist after January 1942, and also because at no time had such plans been made.

So it was that when the fleet and the convoy of 'Operation Pedestal' sailed through the Straits of Gibraltar on the 10th of August, the 'Target Date', as it was called, by which capitulation would have been forced on the military commands by a breakdown of food and fuel supplies, lay between the 31st of August and the 7th of September, unless a fair proportion of the convoy's cargo could be unloaded at Malta.

Further delay in surrendering would have meant widespread death from starvation among the quarter of a million Maltese civilians, the 18,000 regular troops and the 8,000 Maltese serving with the colours on the Island.

All depended on this operation. If it had failed it

would have been impossible to arrange another convoy in time; and even if a small part of 'Pedestal', say only two ships, had won through, it is still doubtful whether it would have been feasible to arrange another before starvation compelled the defenders to strike the Union Jack from the staff above the Residency, where it had flown defiantly for so many difficult and dangerous months.

That Malta's plight was desperate at this time is common property, though the narrow margin by which it was saved was known only to the few immediately concerned with the Island's defence and to the leaders of the British war effort at this time. Why no evacuation had ever been considered and why no attempt to save so many seasoned troops and much valuable material had been planned is, however, something of a historical mystery.

The difficulty of holding Malta under foreseeable circumstances of Mediterranean war had been recognized since 1914. Despite the determination of the War Cabinet to hang on to the Island at any price and the efforts made to implement this determination, the stark reality of earlier forecasts must have been evident long before the beginning of 1942, when the surrender date was forecast in months, then weeks and then days.

Why then had no evacuation plan been produced? The reason probably lay in the difficulty of such an operation. The threat of the Italian fleet had been in no way diminished by British naval successes in the Mediterranean, which were offset by our heavy losses there and in other parts of the world; and the situation was aggravated by the difficulty of assembling a big British fleet with so many commitments elsewhere. Moreover, the risk to fleet elements was probably considered too great to hazard them on what would have been essentially a negative operation; for the Axis held command of the air over the greater part of the sea and the disasters of Greece and Crete had emphasized just how costly such operations could be without air superiority.

Psychologically this absence of plan may be another example of the positivity of thought which underlay the British direction of the war and which constituted the greatest of many qualities which the character of Churchill imparted to the British will to victory.

The British war leader's dislike for thinking in terms of defeat, even though the thought amounted only to the established military practice of providing for all eventualities, is well known.

For instance, Sir John Kennedy, the Director of Military Operations from 1940 to 1943, describes in his book *The Business of War* the storm which broke when Churchill heard of Wavell's 'Worst Possible Case', a general paper on action to be taken in event of failure to check the German advance into Egypt.

The man who, providentially for Britain, believed that war was a contest of wills, flushed and lost his temper. Wavell, Kennedy and the other generals were accused of defeatism in even thinking it was possible to lose Egypt. 'If they lose Egypt, blood will flow. I will have firing parties to shoot generals,' he roared.

Whatever may have been the causes of this absence of plan, the situation progressively deteriorated from January, until, by the spring, any thought of an organized evacuation became impossible. By early summer, with the sinking or removal of most of the naval units from Malta, there were not sufficient ships, yachts or rowing boats in the Island to move 500 men, and the Axis sea and air blockade was such that rescue by the Navy was out of the question as a practical operation.

The Island was thus faced with fighting to the last crust and the last round.

II

After the failure of the March convoy, the Governor
ordered yet another tightening of belts, and the hopes of
the defenders were concentrated on the promised
convoy in May.

On the 18th of April the Chiefs of Staff in London
concluded that, in view of the general naval situation,
to run a convoy to Malta would be out of the question.

This decision profoundly shocked those who were
responsible for the Island's defence. They at once took
stock of the larder, and Sir Edward Jackson, the Deputy
Governor, calculated, from the reports which had been
called for, that only seventy days' supply of wheat and
flour remained.

This too was dependent upon a chance factor, for of
the available stocks only thirty days of this supply was
in flour. The ability to make use of wheat supplies
depended upon the flour mills which were situated in
the docks, the most heavily bombed military target in
the Island. These had already been damaged and had
recently been out of action for several days.

Calculating on the flour index, and stocks and consumption of other vital materials were roughly equiv-
alent to this, it meant that they could not safely count
on being able to hold out for more than thirty days, or at
the most forty, if supplies were stretched to the final
limit.

Without further supplies, in fact, they could hold out
to the end of June at the longest and, if the worst
happened and the flour mills were destroyed, until the
end of May only.

Nor would any small convoy solve the crisis. To live,
the Island required some 26,000 tons of supplies a
month, which amounted to the balanced cargo of about
three large ships. Experience had shown that less than a

quarter of the cargo loaded in any convoy could be expected to reach the Island's underground stores. A ten-ship convoy was the greatest which could conveniently be mustered and escorted, and the extensive preparations needed for mounting so large an operation limited dispatch to a maximum of one every two months. It therefore became evident that, even upon the previous scale of effort, the Island was consuming its stocks quicker than it could be supplied. The end now seemed in sight.

General Dobbie ordered the bread ration to be cut by a quarter and appraised the War Cabinet of the results of their grim calculation.

The situation, he pointed out, had gone beyond the critical stage. 'It is obvious that the very worst may happen if we cannot replenish our vital needs . . . It is a question of survival,' he wrote.

When the Defence Committee met in London again on the 22nd of April, Churchill made it clear that he was not going to allow Malta to fall and that he was prepared to run extreme military risks to save the Island. In this he had the full support of the Admiralty.

The army, however, was less prepared to play what the Prime Minister called 'paying forfeits' in India and the desert to succour Malta; and one result was that General Auchinleck, when told to mount an offensive in the desert to divert attention from the coming Malta convoys, gave the opinion that the retention of the Island was not absolutely necessary to his plans. He was therefore ordered by the Prime Minister to take the offensive.

At this critical Defence Committee meeting, the Prime Minister even discussed bringing four capital ships and three modern cruisers from the Indian Ocean to the Mediterranean via Suez to carry a convoy to the Island, with the additional hope of bringing the Italian fleet to action on the way. This plan was finally shelved, but in principle it was agreed that convoys should be

fought through to Malta at the earliest possible date,
and that a great degree of risk to the naval forces
employed should be accepted.

The service departments, with the assistance of the
Ministry of War Transport, immediately began discussing ways and means of arranging the convoys, but they
were faced with a grave difficulty which had already
presented itself.

The minimum speed at which a Mediterranean
convoy could travel without grave danger to merchant
ships and escort was sixteen knots. Many merchantmen
could be found capable of this speed; but in the available
fleet of British ships, no tanker existed with more than
twelve knots. Yet a tanker had to be included to supply
two of the vital deficiencies from which Malta was
dying; for, although aviation spirit might be loaded in
other vessels, only a tanker could carry a large enough
cargo of oil and kerosene.

At an earlier meeting of the War Cabinet Committee
responsible for organizing the convoys, Sir Ralph Met-
calfe, who was head of the Tanker Division of the
Ministry of War Transport, had been present and had
been asked if he knew any way of solving this
problem.

Sir Ralph agreed that no fast tankers existed in the
British fleet or in any of the available Allied fleets,
except that of the Americans. 'Why not,' he asked, 'try
to borrow one or perhaps two of the American vessels?'
The tanker fleet belonging to the Texas Oil Company
were among the fastest and finest in the world, he
pointed out.

The other committee members shook their heads
doubtfully. They knew that, following Winston Churchill's appeal to Roosevelt, the Americans were making
sustained and generous efforts to fill the gap in British
shipping needs; but tankers, and particularly fast ones,
were few even in the American fleet and urgently needed
by the US services to supply their forces in the Far

—

East. Moreover, the loss of tankers, now that Germany had carried the submarine war across the Atlantic to America, had been extremely heavy.

It was unlikely, therefore, that America could afford to lend Britain any of these valuable ships, particularly for an enterprise involving the extreme danger of a Malta convoy.

However, it was agreed that Sir Ralph should try to obtain two fast tankers from America if he could.

Despite the doubts of the Defence Committee, Sir Ralph calculated that he had a fair chance of achieving his object. Some months before, he had visited America and had met most of the leading shipping people there, including chiefs of Texaco. As a result, he was aware of a tender point in the American conscience which he thought might prove a valuable psychological card to play if negotiations for the tankers proved too difficult.

A previous president of one of the biggest tanker fleets in America had been a personal friend of Goering's and had had a number of his tankers built in Germany. When America entered the war and anti-German feeling began to mount, this fact was looked upon as something of a skeleton in the cupboard. Sir Ralph calculated that a delicate suggestion that refusal to supply the tankers might be construed in Britain as evidence of German partiality among American tanker owners would produce a powerful desire in the US authorities concerned to supply the tankers regardless of the cost.

He therefore cabled Sir Arthur Salter, head of the British Merchant Shipping Mission in Washington, asking him to open negotiations for the tankers and suggesting that this psychological card might be used if negotiations looked like failing.

Sir Arthur had gone to Washington in April 1941 and had already succeeded in smoothing out the difficulties of obtaining the 2,000,000 tons of American shipping earlier requested by Churchill.

Whether the psychological card was in fact played in

the negotiations is not clear, but formal application for the tankers was made through the normal channels on 7 January 1942 and Sir Arthur had talks with Harold Ickes, Minister of Commerce, Admiral Emory S. Land, the American War Shipping Administrator, and with officials of the US Maritime Commission.

Reluctance on the American side to part with the tankers is expressed in a letter from H. Harris Robson, the American General Director of Shipping, sent to the chairman of the US Maritime Commission on 17 January 1942.

High Speed Tankers. With reference to Sir Arthur Salter's letter of 7th January requesting that the Commission place at the disposal of the British two sixteen-knot tankers for Mediterranean service, quite a problem is involved. Through conversation with Mr Salter's office we are informed that what the British really need are sixteen-and-a-half-knot vessels capable of keeping up with convoys of supply ships capable of such speed. The only tankers under the American flag definitely capable of sustaining sea speeds in excess of sixteen knots are the so-called National Defense tankers.

'We are told by Commander Callaghan of the Navy that these ships are urgently required by that Department. Already the Navy have taken over all of that type of vessel in existence and have signified their intention of acquiring those under construction when delivered.'

Despite this and the firm stand by the US Navy Department against releasing the tankers, Sir Arthur Salter's negotiations prevailed. American generosity overcame even their own urgent needs and Sir Arthur was informed late in April that the United States would make available the new 14,000 ton tanker *Kentucky* and, if a further tanker was needed, Texaco's *Ohio*.

III

While the June convoy was assembling and negotiations for the two tankers were proceeding, a change had taken place in the leadership on Malta. General Dobbie, worn down by the long strain and responsibility of governing the Island, had asked to be relieved; and Viscount Gort, then Governor of Gibraltar, flew to Malta to take over his duties.

Gort's first action was to ensure that however many ships of the convoy might be lost on the way, those which did arrive would be unloaded in the minimum time, with the minimum loss of cargo.

His arrangements were practical and far-reaching. Specially picked members of the armed forces in the Island were told off to reinforce the dock labourers and every available lorry or truck was commandeered. One-way traffic routes were arranged and marked with individual coloured signs, illuminated at night in such a way that they were hooded from air observation. All other traffic was banned from these routes during an unloading operation and strict traffic control organized. The lorries themselves were allocated colours, depending on the stores they carried, so that by following their corresponding colour route they would speedily arrive at the appropriate depot. A Maltese policeman travelled in each lorry to prevent pilfering.

The scheme was to come into operation immediately a cargo arrived and would continue day and night without halting until all was safely discharged.

Smoke flares were set up round the harbour so that whenever an air-raid was imminent the whole area could be obscured from the enemy bombers.

Not content with this, Gort ordered a full dress rehearsal of the scheme, which was carried out despite the expenditure of vital fuel, shortly before the convoy started.

The mid-June convoy was conceived on a massive scale, in comparison with previous attempts. If a quarter of the ships reached Malta, the Island's troubles would be over.

It was to be run in two parts. The first, from Gibraltar, consisting of six merchant ships, carrying about 43,000 tons of cargo and including the American tanker *Kentucky*, was to be escorted by Acting Captain C. C. Hardy in the anti-aircraft cruiser *Cairo*, with nine destroyers and four mine-sweepers. Admiral Curteis was in support in the battleship *Malaya*, with the old aircraft-carriers *Eagle* and *Argus*, two cruisers and eight destroyers. This part was given the code-name, 'Operation Harpoon'.

The second part, from Alexandria, was to be made up of no less than eleven merchant ships, with a total cargo of about 72,000 tons. Called 'Operation Vigorous', the merchantmen were to be escorted by Rear-Admiral Vian with seven cruisers and twenty-eight destroyers, in addition to a number of smaller escort craft and mine-sweepers. He was to have no covering force of capital ships, however, because it was found impracticable to transfer further units of the Eastern Fleet to the Mediterranean. The old wireless-controlled target ship *Centurion* sailed with the convoy, mocked up to resemble a new battleship, and the planners hoped that the wide use of land-based aircraft and submarines might make up for the absence of aircraft-carriers.

The convoy from Gibraltar reached the Skerki Bank, nearly two-thirds of the journey, on the evening of the 14th of June, with the loss of one merchantman and with the cruiser *Liverpool* disabled by a torpedo in the engine-room. This was in the face of heavy air attacks, and despite the difficulty experienced by the two slow carriers in flying off aircraft with a light following wind.

—

At 9.30 p.m., Admiral Curteis's supporting force withdrew to the westward, for his capital ships could not be risked in the 'Narrows' between Sicily and North Africa where they would have had no room to manœuvre, leaving only Captain Hardy's anti-aircraft cruiser *Cairo*, and the destroyers and mine-sweepers to care for the convoy.

Off the island of Pantelleria at first light next morning, smoke trails appeared on the northern horizon, and air reconnaissance informed Captain Hardy that a force of two Italian cruisers, supported by destroyers, was no more than fifteen miles away.

Within a few minutes salvoes were falling close to the ships of the convoy and the enemy was sighted. Without hesitation *Bedouin* (Commander B. G. Scurfield) led the fleet destroyers to the attack despite the superiority of the enemy force, while *Cairo* and smaller escorts made smoke to screen the convoy.

The British destroyers, outranged by the enemy cruisers, had to steam for some minutes under heavy fire before they could reply with their main armament of 4.7-inch and 4-inch guns.

Bedouin and *Partridge* were hit and disabled, and the Italian destroyer *Vivaldi* was put out of action with serious internal damage.

Having laid smoke, *Cairo* and four *Hunt*-class destroyers joined in, and Da Zara, the Italian admiral, uncertain of the size of the force shrouded in the smoke screen, withdrew.

So effective was the British attack that he believed 'with absolute certainty' that he was engaging, besides *Cairo*, another cruiser of the *Kenya* class.

The Italian admiral's orders were not, as one might have expected, to destroy the convoy at any price, but to score an Italian victory, even a superficial one, to boost morale and offset the depressing effect of previous reverses.

Just before the battle he received a signal from Supermarina, the Italian Naval High Command, ordering him not to engage superior enemy forces. It was partly because of this signal that he believed the British force to be stronger than it actually was.

His two reconnaissance planes, launched from the cruisers just before they opened fire, gave him no news of what was happening on the other side of the smoke screen. He therefore proceeded to make a wide detour to get a clearer view of his opponents.

The convoy, now protected only by mine-sweepers, was meanwhile heavily bombed. Struck by a stick of three bombs, the merchantman *Chant* crumpled and sank in a few minutes, leaving only a dense column of black smoke boiling out of the sea and rising high into the blue sky.

Then the US tanker, *Kentucky*, was damaged by a near-miss. She was taken in tow by the mine-sweeper *Hebe*, and making only six knots, fell astern of the convoy.

The air attacks continued with the utmost ferocity, and, an hour later, another merchantman, *Burdwan*, narrowly missed and shaken by a stick of bombs, stopped. Sooner than risk the crippled tanker falling into enemy hands, Captain Hardy ordered her to be sunk. This was a tragedy for oil-less Malta, for *Kentucky*, with a fractured main steam-pipe, required only a few hours to repair the damage. *Burdwan* was also scuttled.

The Italian fleet was circling the convoy, trying to come within range of the remaining merchantmen without risking another general engagement. The damaged *Bedouin* was sunk by the Italian cruisers and torpedo bombers.

Instead of six ships, the convoy now only numbered two.

Help was coming. At 14.24, two Beaufort aircraft and four naval Albacores from Malta attacked the enemy fleet. This scratch effort did no damage, but, coinciding as it did with an order from Supermarina for Da Zara to withdraw from the area unless the circumstances of the battle were particularly favourable, it seems to

—

have made up the Italian admiral's mind for him. He immediately retired.

The damaged Italian destroyer, *Vivaldi*, reached Pantelleria, and, while *Troilus* and *Orari* were still thrusting onwards towards Malta with their precious cargoes, Da Zara with the remainder of the Italian fleet entered Naples harbour with all guns trained upwards in token of a naval victory. He had carried out Supermarina's orders to the letter.

It was dark when the convoy reached the partially-swept channel in the Malta mine-field. A fleet minesweeper and three destroyers all struck mines, but made harbour, with the exception of the Polish *Kujawiak* which sank almost immediately. Thus, out of a convoy of six ships, only two reached port, *Troilus* and *Orari*.

Operation 'Vigorous' from the eastward had meanwhile got only as far as the beginning of 'Bomb Alley', the sea corridor between Crete and Cyrenaica, when one merchantman was damaged and another found to be too slow to keep up. The following day (14th of June) a second merchantman had to put in to Tobruk because she hadn't the speed to stay with the convoy. As darkness fell a combined air, E-boat and submarine attack accounted for one further ship sunk and another damaged, reducing the eleven merchantmen to seven. Both the cruiser *Newcastle* and the destroyer *Hasty* had also been damaged by torpedoes. The cruiser reached safety but the destroyer was too badly hit and had to be sunk later by the British forces.

Moreover, before the sun had set, an RAF Maryland had spotted two Italian battleships and four cruisers leaving Taranto and steaming south to intercept what remained of the convoy.

Shortly before 2 a.m. on the 15th, Admiral Harwood, Commander-in-Chief Mediterranean, gave Admiral Vian orders to retire to Alexandria with the convoy and screen.

When dawn broke on the 15th, the Italian fleet, two of their newest battleships, *Vittorio Veneto* and *Littorio*, two heavy and two light cruisers and twelve destroyers, were still at least 200 miles to the north-west of the convoy. Admiral Harwood, therefore, ordered fleet and convoy to turn again towards Malta. But when the enemy continued to sail on a southerly course and began to approach uncomfortably close, the order to retire was again given.

Meanwhile, Malta-based Beaufort aircraft attacked the Italian battleships with torpedoes and hit and disabled the 8-inch cruiser *Trento*. Further attacks followed by American Liberators and other RAF aircraft. Reports now reached Admiral Harwood that both Italian battleships had been torpedoed and he at once ordered the convoy to resume its course for Malta.

The air reports, however, soon indicated that our aircraft had lost touch with the Italian fleet, and Admiral Harwood had to decide if convoy and escort should retire or proceed.

Though the Italian fleet was now retiring, the Axis attacks from the air had reached a murderous pitch, and the cruiser *Birmingham* and the destroyer *Airdale* were both seriously damaged. Once again the cruiser limped home, but the destroyer could not be salved and was sunk by British gunfire. Shortly afterwards another merchantman had to turn back, and the Australian destroyer *Nestor* was also hit and had to be scuttled.

Vian then reported that two-thirds of his ships' ammunition had been expended and that the remainder was disappearing at a dangerously fast rate.

The Commander-in-Chief therefore ordered all ships to return to Alexandria.

On the credit side, *Trento* was sunk by the British submarine *Umbra* and the RAF succeeded in scoring one bomb and one torpedo hit on the battleship *Littorio*.

Nevertheless, the Italian claims to have won a victory though exaggerated, were substantially true. Although the loss of the cruiser *Hermione*, torpedoed returning to Alexandria, five destroyers and six merchantmen sunk

—

and others damaged, would have been a light price to pay for the relief of Malta. It was an unfortunate fact that the two ships which did arrive were loaded with a combined cargo of little more than 15,000 tons. Thanks to the excellent arrangements made for the reception of the convoy at Malta, all supplies were unloaded, but it amounted to much less than a month's ration for the Island. The food situation remained critical and, due to the loss of *Kentucky*, the oil and kerosene shortage became desperate.

The Governor decided that it was time to take the people of Malta into his confidence. The day after the arrival of the two ships, therefore, he broadcast the following message to them:

'I must now break to you what the arrival of only two ships means to us. For some time past we have been short of supplies and further privations lie ahead of us. But let us remember that the most glorious sieges in history have always meant hardships, and without hardships there would be little glory . . .'

Sir Edward Jackson returned to the same theme – after a conference between the Governor, his advisers and a party of food experts who had been sent to the Island – four days later, and what he had to tell the sorely-tried defenders was grimmer still.

'. . . greater privation than we have known hitherto lies ahead of us. We received about 15,000 tons of stores from the two ships which arrived. That is something, and certainly a help, but it is a very small part of what we had hoped for. I have come here this evening to tell you plainly what our arrangements are, and I shall tell you the worst. Our security depends, more than anything else, on the time for which our bread will last.

'So it was that when, after our disappointment over the recent convoys, we sat down to examine our position, we first calculated the time for which our bread could be made to last.

'We knew that our present ration could not be reduced

and it will not be reduced. That calculation gave us a date which I shall call the Target Date, the date to aim at. Our next task was to see how we could make our other vital necessities last to the Target Date. We found that with some things we could not do so without some restrictions in the ration, or without making a wider interval between the issues than we make now. And so you will understand that when a ration is reduced or a wider interval made between the dates of issue, the object is to make these things last, wherever possible, as long as bread will last.

'I cannot tell you what the Target Date is, for if the enemy came to hear of it he would learn something that he would very much like to know, but I can tell you that it is far enough off to give very ample opportunity for fresh supplies to reach us before our present stocks run out . . .'

What the Deputy Governor had said was strictly true. The next convoy was due in mid-August and supplies would last for just about fourteen days after that. If that convoy failed, Malta was lost.

CHAPTER FOUR

Report at Greenock

On the 18th of June the Commander-in-Chief of the Mediterranean fleet cabled the Prime Minister. He said that he was doubtful whether it was worth attempting to run another convoy after the disastrous failure of 'Harpoon-Vigorous'.

Three days later a large tanker, rolling slightly in an oily swell, steamed into the mouth of the Clyde.

Her captain, Sverre Petersen, a former Master-in-Sail from Oslo in Norway, squinted at the green hills of Scotland which he had not seen for many years.

Beside him on the bridge Chief Engineer Bush was taking a breath of fresh air. An unanswered question which had occupied the whole crew through the long voyage across the Atlantic was buzzing in his mind, but he hesitated to ask the usually uncommunicative captain about it.

'Well, we shall be there soon, Chief,' said the captain, without taking his eyes off the undulating coastline.

The engineer took the plunge: 'What's going to happen to us in England, Cap? Shall we see any fun, do you think.'

The Captain shrugged his shoulders. He had sailed in one war already and had been overboard in a hurricane. Whatever happened to be over the horizon at sea would be met in good time without unprofitable speculation.

'Search me,' he replied. 'We're ordered to the Clyde with gasoline. We're here. As far as I'm concerned the rest is rumour. I've not been told what happens after that. Best wait and see.' He lifted his glasses and focused them on another tanker approaching them.

Despite the German U-boats scouring the Atlantic in

search of prey and, as they approached Europe, the drone of long-range German bombers, the voyage of *Ohio* had been uneventful. In fact, from the day of her launching her whole life had been the humdrum existence of an ordinary oil tanker, plying between Port Arthur and various American ports; except that she had once set up a speed record from Bayonne to Port Arthur covering 1,882 miles in 4 days, 12 hours, an average of more than 17 knots.

Then, one day early in May 1942 a radio message had reached the captain, diverting the ship to Galveston, Texas. There was nothing unusual in that, but when he reached port orders awaited Captain Petersen which brought an involuntary whistle to his lips.

Ohio was to proceed to Britain, the first American tanker to visit what had become almost a beleaguered citadel of war. As a foretaste of what might be in store for her, two guns, a 5-inch and a 3-inch AA, were fitted. Then she moved to Sinclair Terminal, Houston, Texas, where she loaded a full cargo of 103,576 barrels of petrol before sailing on the 25th of May.

Ohio discharged her cargo at Bowling on the Clyde, then steamed out into the tideway and anchored, awaiting orders.

Many curious eyes turned towards her as she swung easily in the current. Her long lines with the perceptible sheer were noted, the high bridge amidships and the squat funnel aft. A nice-looking ship, big for a tanker – must be fast. American? What was she doing here in ballast then? No one, least of all the puzzled American crew, seemed to know the answer.

Although *Ohio*'s destiny had already been settled at the highest level between the British and American governments no word of its portent or the means by which it was to be implemented could be allowed to leak out.

There was no clue in the letter received by Captain Petersen on his arrival. This was sent by Lord Leathers, the head of the British Ministry of War Transport, bidding the master a personal welcome '. . . at your safe arrival in the Clyde with the first cargo of oil carried in a United States tanker.'

A telegram received the same day by the head office of Texaco from the US Shipping Administration, therefore, created a sensation and by no means a pleasant one. It announced simply that the *Ohio* was being requisitioned 'pursuant to the law'.

The immediate reaction was a cabled message from Mr T. E. Buchanan, General Manager of Texaco's Marine Department to the firm's London agent, that on no account was *Ohio* to leave her discharging port of Bowling on the Clyde.

The master was told further orders would arrive soon. No one seemed to know what was happening; and, indeed, even the highest British and American authorities were in some doubt as to how the formalities of their concerted action should be carried out: for the circumstances were unique. Then again there was a period of doubt on the British side about using *Ohio* for the momentous operation projected, because of the unusual hazards to which so fine a ship would be subjected.

Two weeks later the decision was finally taken.

A launch sped out to the ship anchored in the Clyde and Texaco's London agent, accompanied by an official of the British Ministry of War Shipping, came over the side.

Captain Petersen received them in his cabin. 'We've got some rather unpleasant news for you, Captain,' the agent explained awkwardly. 'You and your crew will be leaving this ship. She's to be handed over to a British crew.'

'What, hand over my ship? What the blazes do you mean?' roared the captain . . . The agent and the man from the Ministry spent an unpleasant hour. The agent knew no more than the information contained in the apparently outrageous order. The man from the Ministry knew a little more, but was not allowed to explain.

'Some sort of convoy, you say?' asked the captain, by now in the last stages of exasperation. 'Can't an American sail in a convoy as well as a "Limey"?' Scores of later convoys, and indeed previous ones had proved that an American could, but the unexplained orders were final. The captain had no option but to give in.

The crew was no less flabbergasted by the news and received it, understandably, with somewhat bad grace.

Such a transfer was unheard of; the method seemed dictatorial, not to say suspect. After all, what were they supposed to be fighting against but this sort of thing?

Next day strangers began to come aboard; the English seamen who were to take over. Reluctantly the Americans began to pack up and the considerable amount of scramble involved did nothing to improve frayed tempers. It is surprising the amount of gear a seaman can collect on board a ship in two years and no one had enough bags. The chief mate, Ralph Kuhn, had to turn the seamen to making emergency kit-bags to hold it all.

Finally, on the 10th of July, Captain Petersen handed over the ship. There was no formal ceremony and little goodwill. The American flag was run down and *Ohio* thenceforward sailed on her short trip to fame under the 'Red Duster'.

Overnight she was transferred from American to British registry.

For convenience in management *Ohio* was handed over on the 25th of June to the British Eagle Oil and Shipping Company.

Before the transaction was completed the company was warned by the Ministry of War Transport that the tanker was required for a special convoy and that much might depend upon the quality and courage of the crew.

Accordingly a hurried search was made for the best men then available.

Soon, the telephone bell was ringing in a small sub-urban home at Surbiton, Surrey. Captain Mason lifted himself reluctantly from a comfortable armchair, yawned and said to his brother: 'Don't you go, it's probably for me.' Two minutes later he returned to the sitting-room.

'Something's happened,' he said shortly, 'but what it is and what ship, I haven't a clue. It's the usual business. Just report to the Clyde as quickly as possible and no questions.'

Dudley W. Mason at thirty-nine had already held other commands. He was one of the youngest of the Eagle Oil Company's captains and had begun an apprenticeship with the company when he was seventeen years old. He had been on leave, standing by to receive the command of *Empire Norman* which was building. Now it seemed there was another change of plan, but after three years of war he was used to sudden upheavals of this sort and took them philosophically. He went upstairs to pack his bag.

At Euston Station, he met another of the Eagle's masters. He too had been ordered to the Clyde immediately without explanation.

As the train sped northwards, they speculated on the sudden summons and agreed that such a 'gathering of the clans' must mean something big was in store for them.

About the same time on this Sunday afternoon, chief engineer James Wyld, another tried servant of the company, now forty years old, received a telegram at his digs in Belfast where he was supervising the installation of machinery in another tanker, *San Veronica*, at Harland and Wolff's shipyard.

The message read: 'Report Greenock at once.'

Next morning, he was greeted at the company's Glasgow office by the agent, Mr W. L. Nelson.

The agent would say little about the sudden call. 'I'd

just like you to look at a ship, Jimmy,' he said. 'I think
you might like her.'

Together they set out in a launch and boarded *Ohio*.
For more than two hours, the engineer examined the
engines and auxiliary machinery, poked into dark corners and mentally assessed the complicated pattern of
cylinders, pipes, pumps and boilers which make up the
motive power of a modern tanker.

Then he came on deck and looked questioningly at
the agent. 'Well . . .?'

'Would you like to take over the engine-room for a
special job?' asked the agent.

'Blimey, would I not?' said Wyld enthusiastically.
'She's the finest ship I've ever seen.'

Wyld spent the rest of the day gloating over the
machinery and savouring the compliment which was
implied by sending him to so fine a ship. Most of the
American crew had now gone, but the third engineer
had been sporting enough to volunteer to stay behind to
show the English crew the ropes. Wyld took full advantage of this chance to learn something about his new
ship.

That evening Captain Mason came aboard and
received a hearty greeting from Wyld. They were old
friends and had sailed together in *San Arcadio*, when
Mason had been second mate and Wyld third engineer.
On that voyage they had spent most of their spare time
playing crib together. Perhaps they would have a chance
for another game or two . . .

During the next few days the other officers and the
crew began to arrive. But Mason and Wyld saw with
pleasure that they were all young, picked men of the
Eagle fleet.

There was Gray, the chief officer, a quiet, fair-com-
plexioned Scot from Leith, who had packed twelve years
of seafaring into his twenty-six years of life; McKilligan,
a stout, blustery western Highlander of about twenty-
eight years of age, signed on as second mate; Stephen, a

happy-go-lucky twenty-year-old from Dundee was to act as third mate.

In the engine-room the second, Buddle, a fine-drawn Cornishman, with delicate hands and an intelligent face, was the first to join Wyld, followed by Grinstead, the third, a burly South African, older than most of the others, a man of great experience.

Both officers and crew were delighted when chief steward Meeks joined the ship, for this imperturbable Lancashire man was one of the wits of the Eagle fleet and generally popular.

Forty-eight hours after *Ohio* had been transferred to British registry her crew was completed. The ship's company numbered seventy-seven men, an almost unprecedented number for a tanker of this size, and it included no fewer than twenty-four naval and army ratings to serve the guns.

The ship then moved to King George's Dock and was moored under the big crane there. At once a new armament was placed aboard and fitted. This, too, was significant. Besides the 5-inch gun aft and the 3-inch gun in the bows for anti-aircraft defence, both of which had been fitted in America, a 40 mm army Bofors quick-firing gun was bolted to a strong point just abaft the funnel and six 20 mm naval Oerlikons were placed at suitable points round the ship. This was quite a heavy anti-aircraft armament and quite unknown in merchant ships at that period of the war. Half the Oerlikons were manned by the Maritime Regiment of the Royal Artillery and the Royal Navy and the remainder were the responsibility of the crew. Two of the guns on the bridge top were manned by apprentices who thoroughly enjoyed this unusual opportunity to run a real shooting gallery.

By this time speculation on what was to come had reached a high pitch and the most extraordinary rumours were current. No one, however, knew for

certain although Captain Mason had heard a whisper
that Malta was to be their destination.

The day after the guns had been fitted the captain was
resting in his cabin when there was a tap on the door.
A fresh-faced naval lieutenant of about twenty-five
entered.

'Denys Barton, sir. I'm reporting for duty. I'm your
liaison officer, I'm afraid.'

Mason noted with approval the firm mouth relieved
by lines of humour. Barton was obviously nervous and
still standing to attention.

'For God's sake sit down, man, you're in the Merchant
Navy now,' said Mason. 'What do you know? Where are
we going?'

Barton had not long returned from the Eastern Mediterranean after serving aboard an anti-aircraft cruiser.
After seven of the sixty days' leave for which he was due
had passed, he had received a cryptic order to report to
the admiral and was told simply to go to Glasgow and
join *Ohio*.

He shrugged his shoulders: 'Search me,' he said. 'They
never tell you anything at the Admiralty. I suppose we
shall know soon enough.'

As he spoke the cruiser *Nigeria* could be seen coming
to anchor out in the Clyde. They were soon to know the
full hazard of their mission.

CHAPTER FIVE

Pedestal Planned

After the disastrous failure of the mid-June convoy considerable doubt was expressed as to whether it was worth while attempting to supply Malta further. It was questioned if the Island could hold out on the meagre supplies rescued from 'Harpoon-Vigorous' until another convoy could be organized; and if it was possible at all for any convoy to fight through sufficient supplies to build up stocks to a point at which surrender would not be inevitable.

Running a convoy in the brilliance of a Mediterranean moonlit period was to court inevitable disaster and this limited any operations in the immediate future to the moonless period in July or August between the 10th and 16th of those months.

July was out of the question. The tanker *Ohio* could not be fitted out in time, moreover 'Harpoon-Vigorous' had shown that only the most careful planning would be likely to achieve any measure of success, and this would be impossible before the July period. A much heavier escort would be needed than in June, and the requisite heavy units of the fleet which would have to take part could not be assembled in time. Could Malta hold out till August?

The arrival of a more optimistic appraisal of the situation from Lord Gort, estimating a Target Date in September for the exhaustion of supplies, settled the matter.

Churchill and the Defence Committee were determined to try once more to save the Island fortress, and orders were immediately issued for the planning of the great Malta convoy.

The suspension of the North Russian convoys had enabled the Admiralty to draw upon the Home fleet for this operation, so for once there was no great shortage of ships. So that nothing should be lacking to ensure some success for the convoy, all resources and facilities at the Admiralty were placed at the disposal of the Flag Officer who was to command the operation.

The man to whom the responsibility of this great venture fell was a young, clean-shaven South African, Vice-Admiral Sir Neville Syfret, who had succeeded Admiral Sir James Somerville, commanding Force H, the fleet normally operating from Gibraltar in the Western Mediterranean and in the Eastern Atlantic.

Admiral Syfret was on his way home from the successful capture of Diego Suarez, the French colony on the island of Madagascar, when he received a signal to proceed at once to London.

Discussions at the Admiralty were attended also by Rear-Admiral A. L. St G. Lyster, who was to command the carrier force and by Rear-Admiral H. M. Burrough. Admiral Burrough, who had commanded the escort of the successful September convoy to Malta in the previous year, was entrusted with the most difficult job of all, namely the close escort of the merchant vessels throughout their hazardous voyage.

The broad plan which they had been ordered to implement was to escort a fleet of fourteen merchant vessels, including the *Ohio*, from the west to Malta. The War Cabinet had considered sending another convoy through from the east, but this had finally been vetoed. As the previous June convoy had abundantly illustrated, 'Bomb Alley' between Crete and the North African shore, now largely in the hands of the Germans, was suicidal. Not only did the Axis possess almost complete command of the air over this long sea corridor, but the Italian fleet could here concentrate forces superior to any which could be gathered for convoy escort at Alexandria.

The convoy from the west, then, was to be prosecuted relentlessly, with the acceptance of great danger of naval loss, and the determination of the War Cabinet to drive it through irrespective of risk can be measured by the fact that they even considered sending the whole fleet through to Malta.

This plan was finally abandoned owing to the almost certain loss of too great a proportion of heavy fleet units in the 'Narrows'.

The 'Narrows' constituted the gravest problem and the greatest difficulty to the planning and execution of the operation. In fact, this channel between Sicily and Cape Bon, on the African shore, bedevilled the planning of all Malta convoys from the west. It is less than 100 miles wide and obstructed at the western end by the Skerki Bank, an area of shallows. At the eastern end, the Italian-occupied island of Pantelleria was a formidable fort which divided the 'Narrows' in two. Two courses only were therefore open to the planners. The first lay south of the Skerki Bank and round Cape Bon on the edge of French North African territorial waters where the Italians had hitherto laid no mines, then well south of Pantelleria before turning east to Malta. The second involved sailing north of the Skerki Bank and then down the south-west coast of Sicily where Axis coastwise shipping had prohibited the use of mines.

Either course entailed big risks, particularly to capital ships which were unable to manœuvre in these narrow confines; and, owing to the ease with which the Axis could defend such restricted waters, any fleet of ships, large or small, could expect odds heavily weighted against them.

The second course was the shortest but by far the most dangerous, lying as it did within a few seconds' flying of the Sicilian air bases. Admiral Burrough suggested following this bold course, for it had paid him well on the previous occasion in September, when only one ship of the convoy had been lost. The others, however, considered that such surprise tactics were not likely to succeed more than once, and the first course by way of Cape Bon was decided upon.

Against any threat by the Italian fleet to bar the convoy's course in the Western Mediterranean the battleships *Nelson* (wearing the flag of Admiral Syfret) and *Rodney* were to form the principal part of the covering force, called Force Z. These two major fleet units of the same class were the most powerful of the older battleships in the British navy, displacing nearly 34,000 tons each, and each armed with nine 16-inch guns, twelve 6-inch guns and heavy anti-aircraft protection. Both carried 14-inch armour plating.

The chief difference from the June convoy lay in the very heavy support given by no less than three aircraft-carriers. 'Harpoon-Vigorous' had shown that unless strong fighter protection could be given to the fleet heavy losses would inevitably result from the strengthened enemy squadrons stationed in Sardinia and Sicily. The old carriers used in the June convoy had, moreover, proved unsatisfactory owing to their lack of speed. In addition, therefore, to the old *Eagle*, a 22,000 ton heritage of the First World War, the force was stiffened with two of Britain's most modern carriers.

Completed in 1940, *Indomitable*, 23,000 tons, was the last word in aircraft-carrier construction, and among the largest ships of her type afloat. *Victorious*, only a year older and displacing 23,000 tons, was an equally formidable unit. Both were capable of a speed over thirty knots and, with *Eagle*, these two fine vessels were able to put some seventy fighters into the air.

This carrier squadron itself represented a tactical revolution, for it was the first time that three such valuable ships had operated together.

Three cruisers, *Phoebe*, *Sirius* and *Charybdis*, were also to accompany Force Z. These ships belonging to the Dido class had all been completed early in the war, and carried a strong anti-aircraft armament in addition to ten 5·25-inch guns each and six 21-inch torpedo tubes. Though lightly armoured they could call upon a speed of thirty-three knots despite their displacement of 5,450 tons.

Force Z was to be screened by fourteen destroyers of the Nineteenth flotilla commanded by Captain R. M. J. Hutton in *Laforey*. This included six modern destroyers of over 1,800 tons, each armed with six 4·7-inch guns and also 4-inch AA armament.

Close escort for the convoy was to be supplied by Force X commanded by Rear-Admiral Burrough of the Tenth cruiser squadron.

The squadron consisted of *Nigeria*, wearing Admiral Burrough's flag, and *Kenya*, both built in 1939, capable of thirty-three knots with a displacement of 8,000 tons, and a primary armament of twelve 6-inch guns and eight 4-inch AA guns; *Manchester*, 9,400 tons, two years older and armed with twelve 6-inch guns; and the 4,000 ton *Cairo*, an old ship reconditioned in 1939 as an anti-aircraft cruiser mounting eight 4-inch AA guns.

They were to be accompanied by the Sixth destroyer flotilla, commanded by Acting Captain R. Onslow in the Tribal class destroyer *Ashanti* with an armament of six 4·7-inch guns and two 4-inch AA guns, and ten other destroyers.

The strong force of cruisers which was thus to accompany the convoy through the 'Narrows' to Malta also represented a lesson learned from the June attempt, and this time the Italian Navy would not be able to attack them with impunity after the main force had turned back.

After considerable discussion, it was decided that Force Z should return westward on reaching the Skerki Bank, the last position at which the main fleet could manœuvre safely.

This vital moment of the operation was timed for 7.15 p.m. on the 12th of August when dusk would fall over the Mediterranean. This would enable Force X to pass through the most dangerous part of the Sicilian channel in darkness. For the convoy and her close escort the most dangerous time would be at dawn on the 13th, when the most favourable circumstances for an attack by the Italian fleet would exist. By then, however, long-range air cover could be expected from Malta, and this would increase as the convoy progressed to the eastward. To obtain the maximum co-operation from the Malta-based aircraft, both *Nigeria* and *Cairo* were fitted with very high frequency radio telephone, over which the escort could talk to and direct the pilots.

During the passage from the Straits of Gibraltar, which were to be passed at midnight on the 10th, the chief danger was from enemy aircraft, but it was hoped that the formidable anti-aircraft protection afforded by the combined fleet and the strong fighter escort which the carriers were capable of putting up would be sufficient to repel the fiercest enemy attacks.

Eight submarines were also to take part in the operation. Two were to patrol to the north of Sicily off Palermo and Milazzo, while the other six were given patrol lines south of Pantelleria, which they were to take up at dawn on the 13th of August. As the convoy passed their patrol lines the submarines were to proceed on the surface to act as a screen. It was hoped that they might be spotted by enemy aircraft and that reports of their position would deter the Italian fleet from setting out. If the Italian fleet was sighted the submarines were allowed complete freedom of action and were ordered to attack the Italian battleships and cruisers.

Fleet, convoy and escort, when together were referred to as Force F.

At the last minute, wastage of Spitfires at Malta began to cause alarm and another operation known as 'Bellows' was arranged. *Furious*, the 22,400 ton aircraft-carrier, was to accompany the fleet until within about 550 miles of Malta when she would fly 38 Spitfires off to join the Island's defence.

Arrangements were also made for refuelling the lighter escort ships both from tankers at sea in the Mediterranean and from Gibraltar.

Although a breakthrough to Malta from Alexandria was now considered too dangerous, two dummy operations were to be mounted from there in the hope of preventing the enemy from throwing the full weight of his surface and air forces against the main convoy from the west. Admiral Harwood had orders to put to sea with three cruisers, ten destroyers and three merchant ships on the 10th of August, and to sail in the direction of Malta. The day after, Admiral Vian, with two cruisers, five destroyers and one merchant ship was to sail from Haifa. After joining up, the two forces were to proceed towards the west until dusk on the 11th, when they were to turn back and disperse.

The Royal Air Force at Malta, commanded by Air Vice-Marshal Sir Keith Park, with reinforcements from the United Kingdom and from Egypt, were now able to put 136 fighters (apart from the reinforcement from 'Bellows') and 38 bombers and torpedo bombers into the air in support of 'Operation Pedestal'. Another 16 aircraft were available for spotting purposes. These aircraft had been allotted a number of different duties.

The torpedo-striking force was to be held to intercept the Italian fleet if it left Taranto to attack the convoy. The remaining aircraft were to combat enemy air forces from Sicily, Sardinia and Pantelleria. Their duties were first and foremost shadowing enemy fleet movements, then protecting 'Pedestal', destroying the enemy's surface fleet if it put to sea, and also bombing enemy aircraft on the ground. Liberators based in the Middle East, were also to take part in these spoiling bombing raids.

While the orders were being made out to implement these naval plans, the Ministry of War Transport was gathering a fleet of some of the best cargo ships afloat.

Three of the largest, *Empire Hope*, 12,700 tons; *Wair-angi*, 12,400 tons; and *Waimarama*, 11,100 tons, belonged to the Shaw Savill & Albion Co., Ltd, of London. These ships had been designed for the South African run, to carry both cargo and passengers, and were all exceptionally fast. There were also two Blue Star cargo liners, *Melbourne Star*, 12,800 tons; and *Brisbane Star*, 11,100 tons. *Dorset*, a 10,600 tonner, came from the Federal Steam Navigation Co., Ltd, and the 9,000 ton *Glenorchy* from the Glen Line Ltd, the big Scottish firm. Four others, though smaller, were among the fastest and best-equipped vessels in the British Mercantile Marine. They were *Port Chalmers*, 8,500 tons, belonging to the Port Line Ltd.; the Union Castle mail ship *Rochester Castle*, 7,800 tons; the Blue Funnel Line's *Deucalion*, 7,500 tons; and the Scottish *Clan Ferguson*, 7,300 tons.

The United States contributed two of their most modern merchantmen to the convoy, besides *Ohio*. Both were leased for the occasion to the Ministry of War Transport. They were the 8,300 ton Grace Line *Santa Elisa*, and *Almeria Lykes*, 7,700 tons, belonging to Lykes Brothers Steamship Company.

Unlike *Ohio*, these ships retained their American officers and men, who were to fight valiantly beside their British allies during the course of the convoy.

Santa Elisa was a last-minute addition. After bringing military stores to Britain, she had partially loaded at Newport, Mon., for the return journey to America. On the 16th of June, however, the orders were counter-manded suddenly and the cargo taken out of her. It was not until the 24th of June that she reloaded with a 'Malta' cargo, arriving with this at Greenock to join 'Pedestal' on the 31st of July.

Almeria Lykes had already been earmarked for the convoy when she arrived with army stores at Belfast. She loaded there without incident and proceeded to Greenock.

—

Most of the other vessels loaded at Gourock or Birkenhead and, with the Americans, they carried a grand total of 85,000 tons of cargo. With inevitable losses in view, the Ministry allocated a mixture of Malta's vital needs to each ship with the exception of kerosene and fuel oil. The bulk of supplies loaded was flour, but each ship carried a percentage of petrol and aviation spirit in tins and also shells and other explosives.

Ohio sailed down to Dunglass in the Clyde and loaded 11,500 tons of kerosene and diesel fuel oils. She was the only ship carrying these supplies which were so vital to the survival of Malta.

Before she sailed, however, special strengthening was given to the tanker to protect her against the shock of bombs exploding in the sea close to her. In the previous convoy, *Kentucky* had had to be sunk with only a few hours' repair work needed on a steam-pipe, which had been broken by the force of such explosions. The Ministry was determined that this should not happen again, so *Ohio*'s engines were mounted on rubber bearings, to reduce shock, and all steam-pipes were supported with steel springs and baulks of timber.

While the merchant ships were gathering in the Clyde, the naval forces had already reached Scapa Flow. Admiral Syfret joined *Nelson* there on the 27th of July and held a final conference with Flag and Commanding Officers on the 29th, at which arrangements for the operation were gone through in detail. Orders were then given for the fleet to proceed to the mouth of the Clyde to pick up the convoy.

CHAPTER SIX

We Shall Not Fail . . .

Captain Mason of *Ohio*, or *O.H.*10 as the new crew persisted in calling her, climbed the gangway of the cruiser *Nigeria* followed by Lieutenant Denys Barton, his naval liaison officer.

All leave had been stopped on that day, the 2nd of August, and the convoy conference they were about to attend would end all rumours and speculations. After two weeks of waiting they would be told the worst or the best of their mission.

They were shown into the aircraft hangar of the cruiser, a large bare box of steel perched high up amidships. On chairs set out on the armour-plated deck the masters, and liaison and radio officers of the convoy were shifting impatiently and whispering to one another in low voices.

As they sat down at the rear of the throng, Barton nudged his new captain (he had just been signed on in *Ohio* as a deck-hand at a wage of a shilling a month, to satisfy Board of Trade rules).

'Is it going to be South Africa, then?' he whispered, pointing to the blackboard on which the convoy number was set out – 'WS21S'. The convoy prefix 'WS', nick-named 'Winston's Specials', stood for the South African route from England round the Cape of Good Hope by which Suez and the Desert Army were usually supplied.

At this moment Rear-Admiral Burrough, craggy and smiling, entered the hangar with Commander A. G. Venables, the retired naval officer who was to act as Commodore of the convoy in the merchant ship *Port Chalmers*, and other executive officers.

The admiral threw down a sheaf of papers on the steel

table facing the expectant men, and in the tense hush the sound echoed through the hangar.

The admiral cleared his throat: 'Well, you're going to Malta,' he said.

Suppressed whistles and confused murmurings came from his audience. The admiral looked at the board: 'Don't bother about the convoy number,' he said. 'That's just to confuse the Hun in case he hears about it. You're going to Malta all right, by way of Gibraltar. The operation is to be called "Pedestal".'

Orders for the convoy were given. For two hours the master and their liaison officers listened while various executive officers gave the details of convoy positions, signals for emergency turns, for air-raids and for almost every other foreseeable emergency which might be expected during the voyage.

Finally, each of the masters was given a sealed, official-looking envelope marked: 'Not to be opened until under way.'

The admiral stood up, ending the conference. 'There it is, gentlemen,' he said. 'By the 12th of August we should be on the edge of the Skerki channel. You know what the 12th is. That's the day grouse shooting starts and we should have plenty of birds in the Mediterranean.'

The admiral raised his hand and the burst of laughter died.

'We sail tonight, so it's time you went aboard,' he said. 'That's the lot . . . except, good luck.'

With a sharp tattoo of boots on the steel deck the seamen bustled to the door, red, sunburned faces animated with excitement and enthusiasm. They might have been schoolboys off for the holidays rather than commanders of vital ships in what, at best, was bound to be a grim and hazardous enterprise.

Soon the waters of the Clyde were busy with the picket boats, launches and other craft taking them back to their ships.

Aboard *Ohio*, the officers had somehow contrived to

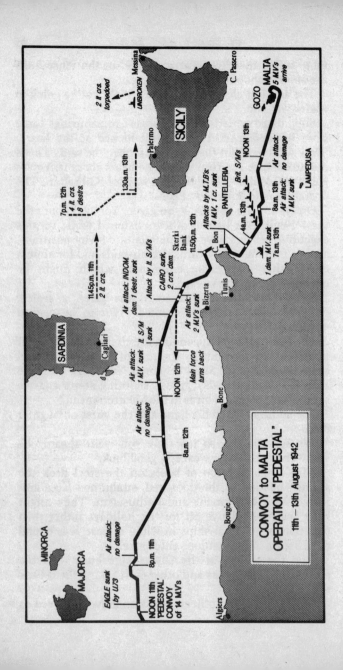

CONVOY to MALTA
OPERATION "PEDESTAL"
11th – 13th August 1942

MINORCA

MAJORCA

EAGLE sunk by U/73

NOON 11th 'PEDESTAL' CONVOY of 14 MV's

8p.m. 11th — Air attack: no damage

Air attack: no damage — 8a.m. 12th

Air attack: 1 M.V. sunk

NOON 12th

Main force turns back

Air attack: 2 MV's sunk

SARDINIA

Cagliari

11.45p.m. 11th — 2 lt. crs.

Air attack: INDOM. dam. 1 destr. sunk

Attack by It. S/M's

CAIRO sunk, 2 crs. dam.

Sterki Bank

11.50p.m. 12th

It. S/M sunk

7p.m. 12th — 4 lt. crs. 8 destrs.

1.30a.m. 13th

Palermo

SICILY

Messina

UNBROKEN

2 lt crs torpedoed

C. Bon

1 dam. M.V. sunk — 7a.m. 13th

Attacks by M.TB's: 4 M.V. 1 cr. sunk

4a.m. 13th

1 M.V. sunk — 4a.m. 13th

8a.m. 13th Air attack: 1 M.V. sunk

PANTELLERIA

Brit. S/M's

NOON 13th

Air attack: no damage

LAMPEDUSA

C. Passero

GOZO

MALTA
5 MV's arrive

Tunis

Bizerta

Bone

Algiers

Bougie

be loitering near the gangway when Captain Mason and
Lieutenant Barton returned.

'Well, where is it to be?' asked the first officer as they
strolled towards the bridge. Mason grinned. 'Malta, I'm
afraid,' he said.

Two minutes later the tale was all round the ship.

At 8 p.m. that evening, two hours before dusk, the
convoy sailed. Slowly and hesitantly at first, with some
manœuvring, the fourteen ships, led by HMS *Nigeria*,
formed up. It was dark by the time they reached the
open sea.

As the light grew in the east next day, a memorable
sight greeted the watches on duty. On both sides of the
convoy, strung out in two long lines, the grey shapes of
warships heaved in the light swell of the Irish Sea. There
were destroyers and cruisers, and away astern the two
great 'battle wagons', *Nelson* and *Rodney* followed
sedately like governesses behind a school crocodile.
Overhead Sunderland aircraft of RAF Coastal Command
weaved to and fro scanning the seas for enemy
submarines.

On board *Ohio* the men were getting used to their
new quarters. The comparative luxury of the American
way of life afloat after the austerity of ships of their own
Lines was still the subject of awed comment. The petty
officers' and crews' mess-rooms seemed palatial. Since
the British crew had also 'inherited' the stores on board,
the feeding too attained a peak of unaccustomed excel-
lence. At their first meal aboard they stared in unbeliev-
ing amazement at the row of eleven varieties of sauces
on the mess table.

In the second dog-watch that day, all hands were
called to the crew mess-room over the communications
system.

When they had settled themselves, Captain Mason
held up a letter bearing the Admiralty crest, the 'sealed
orders' he had received at the end of the convoy
conference.

'This letter, men, is from the First Lord of the Admiralty, Mr A. V. Alexander,' he said. 'I'll read it to you.'

It read: 'Before you start on this operation the First Sea Lord and I are anxious that you should know how grateful the Board of Admiralty are to you for undertaking this difficult task. Malta has for some time been in great danger. It is imperative that she should be kept supplied. These are her critical months, and we cannot fail her. She has stood up to the most violent attack from the air that has ever been made; and now she needs your help in continuing the battle. Her courage is worthy of yours.

'We know that Admiral Syfret will do all he can to complete the operation with success, and that you will stand by him according to the splendid traditions of the Merchant Navy. We wish you all Godspeed and good luck.'

Without further introduction, the captain told them much of what had passed at the convoy conference the day before. Then he detailed gun and ammunition parties which had been arranged so that 28 gunners from the crew would be on call at any time of the day or night.

When the orders had been given, he paused, packed up his papers and then turned again to the crew.

'You men have been specially chosen for this voyage,' he said. 'You probably wouldn't choose it yourself, but just remember that you are chosen men. I want no dodgers, no questions asked when an order is given. If you are called upon to do extra duties just remember this is a special voyage and one of enormous importance. I don't expect it's going to be a picnic, but just look outside and you'll see the sort of escort we've got. We're not going to have any trouble getting there – there might be a raid or two – but just remember: we're going to get there.

'I've no doubt whatsoever that you will keep up the

traditions of the Merchant Service, if the occasion
demands. I have the utmost faith in you all.'

Captain Mason watched them as they filed out to
their various duties. He knew by the ragged cheering
which had followed his talk, by the mock humorous
misery, the jokes and above all the easy confidence with
which his words had been received, that he had a good
crew. These men would not let him down in an emergency. The naval and military gunners who had been
put aboard for the trip were a tough, reliable-looking lot.
The army Bofors crew, he had heard, had escaped from
Dunkirk as a team and were still together.

The convoy was now steaming in fog and *Lamerton*, a
destroyer, was damaged in collision and had to return to
port. Later that day there was another accident. A
Sunderland flying boat, appearing suddenly out of the
fog, was taken as hostile and shot down into the sea
where it blew up. The destroyer *Ledbury* raced to the
spot and many of her crew went over the side in an
effort to rescue the airmen. Only one was alive when he
was brought aboard.

There were no other untoward incidents in the voyage
down to Gibraltar, but day after day the ships of the
convoy were kept drilling and manœuvring in preparation for the dangers to come, while the anti-aircraft
gunners were long at practice.

Most of the masters and mates were accustomed to
wallowing along in convoy at 8-10 knots and, at first,
they felt some trepidation about carrying out complicated convolutions at sixteen knots. A day of trials,
however, reassured them.

For the first time, in 'Operation Pedestal' no effort had
been spared to concert the movements of the merchant
ships. A naval signalling staff of three had been allocated
to each vessel. Previously a Watch officer had been
expected to decode a string of flags while trying to avoid
a destroyer racing out to depth-charge a submarine or
keep clear of other ships scattered by a bombing raid. It

had often proved too much for him. The merchant ships now were also able to talk to each other and to the commodore of the convoy over a short-range radio telephone. By this means also they would receive early warning of any attack and this assurance built up considerable confidence. Usually the first thing a convoy captain knew about any unexpected happening, or an emergency, was when the depth-charges started to explode, or worse, the ship was torpedoed.

By the time the convoy had drawn abreast of the coast of Spain the ships were manœuvring with speed and ease. Their efficiency drew forth the comment from Admiral Burrough that their zigzags and emergency turns had the efficiency of a fleet unit.

In the merchantmen, the men not engaged in routine duties about the ship were busy preparing for action, for there were many minor details to be attended to.

Aboard *Ohio*, for instance, Pumpman Collins, who had been detailed as a spotter and an ammunition supply man to the Bofors emplacement, found that there was no means of hoisting ammunition up to the gun. So he constructed a hoist out of piping which looked just like an old-fashioned gibbet. He was christened 'The Hangman' after that.

Before fleet and convoy entered the Straits of Gibraltar on the 10th, another operation had been planned called 'Berserk'. This was nothing less than a combined manœuvre of the convoy and the full fleet, under the same conditions which they might expect to meet in the Mediterranean. It began with trials for the aircraft-carriers out in the Atlantic. As this was the first time as many as three carriers had operated as a squadron, it was considered that the benefits of a period working together would far outweigh any danger of the enemy being alerted by the increase in wireless telegraphy and the very high frequency telephony necessary.

Rear-Admiral Lyster sailed in *Victorious* on the 31st of July with *Sirius*, *Argus* and four destroyers from Scapa

Flow to rendezvous with *Eagle and Charybdis* from
Gibraltar. *Indomitable* with *Phoebe* joined the squadron
from Freetown. For two days the three giant capital
ships raced in consort through sharp Atlantic seas
manœuvring and flying off aircraft. The naval pilots
were also practised in flying high and low cover patrols
and in landing on the carriers in conditions of dusk and
darkness. When the operation had been completed to
Admiral Lyster's satisfaction the squadron turned to join
Admiral Syfret's force and the convoy west of Gibraltar.

Early on the 9th the carriers with their escorts were
sighted by the convoy and immediately stations were
taken for a final tactical practice.

First of all fleet and convoy formed up in the cruising
dispositions which would be employed from Gibraltar
to the 'Narrows'. The merchant ships sailed in four
columns, six cables – three-quarters of a mile – apart.
The anti-aircraft cruiser *Cairo* led them and *Kenya*
brought up the rear with *Nigeria* and *Manchester* flank-
ing the merchant ships of the two wing columns.

The battleships, *Rodney* and *Nelson* were placed on
each side of the rear ships in the convoy. Two of the
Hunt-class destroyers were stationed on either beam to
provide close anti-aircraft defence.

A destroyer screen of twenty ships was cast completely round the convoy at a distance of about two
miles with two reserve destroyers in the rear to fill gaps
caused by destroyers leaving the screen to investigate
submarine contacts.

The four aircraft-carriers (*Furious* had joined Admiral
Syfret on the 7th) operated independently inside the
screen each with an escort of one unattached destroyer.
In the event of any of them having to leave the screen to
fly off or take in aircraft two of the nearest destroyers
were ordered to augment their escort. *Victorious*, whose
fighters were mostly the slower Fulmars, was responsible for providing low cover over the fleet. *Indomitable*
and *Eagle* with Hurricanes and Martlets flew a high

cover at 20,000 feet, and each carrier was responsible for supplying its own protective air patrol. During the Mediterranean passage these were to be maintained from dawn to dusk.

In this order, fleet and convoy carried out emergency turns, zigzag patterns and other group movements while Fleet Air Arm aircraft made practice more realistic by carrying out dummy attacks from all quarters.

The merchantmen and Admiral Burrough's close escort then went through the tricky operation of moving into two columns, a manœuvre which would be necessary on passing into the Skerki channel. It was carried out with complete precision. Then, with a cruiser ahead and astern of each line of merchant ships, four destroyers ahead and one astern, and three on either quarter, convoy and escort proceeded to carry out various forms of evasive action. Moving into a single line of convoy was also tried with good results.

Selected types of the aircraft used by the carriers were then flown slowly over the convoy so the gunners would have an opportunity to recognize them again even in the heat of action.

The final tests having been carried out satisfactorily, many of the smaller naval ships left for Gibraltar to refuel.

As a last reminder of the vital importance of their mission, Admiral Syfret sent the following signal to all ships: 'The garrison and people of Malta, who have been defending their island so gallantly against incessant attacks by the German and Italian air forces, are in urgent need of replenishments of food and military supplies.

'These we are taking to them and I know that every officer and man in the convoy and its escort will do his utmost to ensure that they reach Malta safely.

'You may be sure that the enemy will do all in his power to prevent the convoy getting through and it will require every exertion on our part to see that he fails in

—

his attempt. During the next few days all ships will be in the first and second degree of readiness for long periods. When you are on watch be especially vigilant and alert, and, for that reason, when you are off duty, get all the sleep you can.

'Every one of us must give of his best. Malta looks to us for help. We shall not fail them.'

With these words to occupy their minds, the men of fleet and convoy set course for Gibraltar just as night fell to hide them from the prying eyes of the enemy.

The final bid to save Malta had begun.

CHAPTER SEVEN

The Axis Prepares

On the night of the 10th of August, the convoy with the supporting fleet passed into the Mediterranean in three groups. As they approached the Straits of Gibraltar in the dusk a thick white fog began to form and hopes were high that this, the mightiest fleet ever to sail to Malta, might be well set upon its journey before the Axis was aware of its presence.

As the warships and the attendant merchantmen sailed blind upon a course taking them between the Rock of Gibraltar and Cape Spartel on the African coast, scores of will-of-the-wisp lights began to appear ahead, diffused into soft balls of luminescence by the fog.

Soon the British ships were passing between these lights, and it could be seen that they were Spanish fishing vessels strung out across the Straits. These boats, with their upcurving bows, each with its spluttering naphtha flare at night, were a common sight in the Mediterranean. But was it by chance that on this of all occasions, when a rare fog hid the Straits from watchers on the shore, that they were conveniently placed so as not to miss any number of ships entering the Mediterranean? It was probably an unfortunate coincidence, but Admiral Syfret noted in his log that the enemy would probably be notified of his passage by their agents in Spain.

News of the convoy did in fact quickly reach Germany from across the Pyrenees. Throughout the war, a mass of information passed to and fro between Madrid and Berlin, not only through an efficient system of German agents in Spain, but even from official Spanish sources via the German Legation.

This network had been created by that enigmatic figure Admiral Canaris, head of the German Abwehr or Secret Service. The admiral had close and intimate dealings with many prominent Spaniards and visited the country frequently until 1943, when British pressure (and Allied successes) succeeded in having him barred from crossing the frontier.

Canaris knew Franco and dealt regularly with him through the dictator's brother-in-law, Suner. He was also a personal friend of his opposite number in Spain, General Vignon, and of the shipping magnate Baron de Sacrelirio.

So it had not been difficult to establish at Algeciras early in the war a special observation post manned by German Abwehr agents. This worked solely on behalf of the German navy, observing Allied ships moving through the Straits and operating in and out of Gibraltar.

There were also other German agents near Gibraltar at the time. At Huelva, for instance, a particularly active one was known to British counter-espionage. Between them all an incredible amount of valuable naval information was gathered and transmitted to the Fatherland, particularly from Spaniards who went to work each day on the Rock, returning home at night to Spanish territory.

Despite attempts to mislead spies by dummy movements of ships, little went unnoticed.

A party of young naval officers from Gibraltar, for instance, was dining in Algeciras one night. At the table next to them, another gay gathering from the German Embassy was enjoying neutral hospitality and perhaps a more than prudent amount of Spanish champagne. As the British rose to leave, one of the Germans smiled and said in broken English: 'Tomorrow we see you. You sail out and you sail back, you sail out and you sail back. Then you truly sail out and don't come back. Then we go out and get you.'

Since a large number of the shorter-endurance warships taking part in 'Operation Pedestal' refuelled at
Gibraltar, it was hardly likely that this greatly increased
activity would have passed unnoticed.

In fact, enemy records show that vague information
about the convoy reached Admiral Weichold, the
German Naval Commander-in-Chief, Mediterranean, as
early as the end of July. He had been informed by
Intelligence that a 'large-scale Allied operation was
about to break in the Mediterranean. Large merchant
ships and fleet units were being fetched from far and
wide in preparation'.

As early as the 4th of August, it was known that at
least one aircraft-carrier was joining the convoy as a
protection against submarines and dive-bombing
attacks. At about the same time, the Italian Naval High
Command came to the conclusion from intercepted
reports that the British were preparing an important
Mediterranean operation.

This intelligence must have been partly based on the
activities of the convoy and escorting fleet as it was
approaching Gibraltar on the 9th of August, when
dummy attacks were carried out on the fleet by fleet
fighters followed by a fly past of all carrier-borne aircraft
to help the convoy gunners to identify them during the
following action. This was the first time that so many
carriers had operated in company at sea and a great deal
of wireless telegraphy and plain language wireless
telephony resulted. That much of this would be picked
up by the enemy listening stations was not lost on the
Admiralty planners, but the risk was accepted and
subsequent events showed that it was more than com-
pensated for by the benefit derived by the convoy and
carriers from the practice.

The first definite news of the assembling of a convoy
reached the Italian navy on the same day from an agent
in Ceuta.

It seems possible however that news of the preparation of a Malta convoy had reached the enemy before the British ships had even left Britain.

The suggestion that there had been a serious leakage of information from the United Kingdom was made by Admiral of the Fleet Lord Cork and Orrery, in the House of Lords on 14 October 1942. He said he had been told that some of the cargo loaded on the public docks had been labelled 'Malta'. Though a subsequent enquiry of the Ministry of War Transport seems to have been inconclusive, two naval officers taking part in the 'Pedestal' convoy drew the attention of the Admiralty to loopholes in the security arrangements.

In his report of the operation, Lieutenant-Commander S. W. F. Bennets pointed out that charts of the Mediterranean were openly issued to HM ships before the convoy sailed from England and that the destination, Malta, had been a free topic of public house conversation.

The convoy commodore sailing in *Port Chalmers*, Commander A. G. Venables, also reported that security had in his opinion been weak. He suggested that a smaller convoy, apart from greater ease in manœuvring, would have enabled leakages of information during loading to have been suppressed. 'I joined *Port Chalmers* at Liverpool,' he wrote, 'and was astonished to be told that the ship was bound for Malta. This information was given me by the stevedores.'

To some extent it was impossible to hide the destination of a convoy from stevedores. The nature of a cargo and the way it was packed could be as revealing as a clearly-written label. Human nature being what it is, even the war-long propaganda about careless talk had failed to prevent the discussion of topics of this sort.

It seems possible, therefore, that information may have been passed to the Germans from agents in Britain, and certain that by the morning of the 11th as the

convoy steamed out of the fog into an empty Mediterranean, the enemy knew that it was bound for Malta
and had a good estimation of its strength.

Axis naval experts were able to predict the likely
course of the convoy with considerable accuracy. They
had had previous experience of a large-scale British
attempt to revictual Malta in the mid-June convoy.
Moreover, the sea-room in the 'Narrows' restricted any
breakthrough to the Eastern Mediterranean to one of
two courses: that running close to the African shore
round Cape Bon or that down the north-west coast of
Sicily.

The enemy rightly guessed that the 'Pedestal' convoy,
about which they had had so much detailed information,
would use the Cape Bon route, but their final dispositions allowed for an easy switch to the more northerly
route should that have been necessary.

With ample time to concert arrangements, their plans
produced the best example of Italo-German co-operation
ever achieved during the war in a combined operation.

Early on the 11th of August the Italian submarine
Uarsceik sighted the fleet and reported its make-up and
position, then sixty miles south of Ibiza in the Balearic
Islands.

By this time the Axis submarines had already taken
up their patrol lines. Eighteen Italian submarines were
cruising along the expected route of the convoy between
the meridian of two degrees east, roughly running
through Barcelona in Spain and Algiers in North Africa,
and the Sicilian 'Narrows'.

Eight of these were spread out in search formation
north-east and north-west of Algiers covering an area
which ensured that the convoy would be sighted not
long after its entry into the Mediterranean.

Specific orders had been given to the three German
submarines available for the operation, U.33, U.73 and
U.205. They were to penetrate the destroyer screen and
attempt to sink the aircraft-carriers. They were strung

out in a line, twenty miles apart, north and south of the expected convoy route on Meridian 2° East.

The remaining ten Italian submarines were cruising in positions between Galita Island and Cape Bon, effectively corking the bottle-neck of the 'Narrows'.

All submarine commanders had been carefully briefed on the approximate time and position of projected air attacks on the convoy, so that they could play their part in a combined action. Before the air strikes they had been told to show themselves on the surface at a safe distance, so that the British destroyers would be tempted to break out of the screen to attack them, thus decreasing the anti-aircraft fire-power available to meet the beginning of each air attack. During and after the air attacks, they were ordered to close in again and catch the British forces when they were still spread out providing anti-aircraft cover for the convoy.

Previous experience had shown that British supply ships frequently used French territorial waters, close to the Cape Bon peninsula, as a means of breaking through the Sicilian channel. So, to close the bottle-neck still further, the Italians laid a mine barrage between Cape Bon and Kelibia. These mines were fitted with sterilizers to destroy them after an interval, so that this stretch of French waters would not permanently be endangered, for at this time Axis policy was directed towards wooing Vichy France into closer co-operation.

The Axis naval staffs were able to calculate that by the night of the 11th–12th of August, whatever might remain of the convoy would have reached the area south of Cape Bon between the island of Pantelleria and the North African coast. Here they stationed a total of nineteen Italian E-boats of Nos. 2, 15, 18 and 20 Flotillas, supported by four boats of the German 3rd Flotilla.

These light unarmoured craft, carrying only torpedoes and small calibre automatic weapons, were no match for destroyers. Moreover, the force included six new E-boats of a larger design which had only entered the service a few days before and were considered to be insufficiently worked up for battle.

The Axis planning staff knew however that the British could not commit their heavy units farther east than the 'Narrows' because of the restricted sea room, as previously explained, and hoped that the combined submarine and air attack would succeed in thinning down the number of lighter escorts and scattering the convoy.

It was reasonable therefore to suppose that, under cover of darkness and making use of their high speed, the E-boats would be able to deliver a shrewd blow to the disorganized fleet, a forecast which events proved to be more than justified.

The main Axis attack against the convoy was to be delivered by the Italo-German air forces, and here, too, the concerted plans met with a higher degree of success than in any other of their combined operations.

According to Admiral Weichold, German Naval Commander in Rome, the Sicilian and Sardinian aerodromes had been packed with a total of 540 serviceable aircraft. German bombers, of the II and X Luftflotte numbered 150 with 50 fighters to support them, and there were 130 Italian bombers, 90 of them torpedo-carrying, with a fighter cover of 150 machines. The remaining 60 were presumably reconnaissance machines.

Captured Italian papers suggest numbers as high as 750, but this was probably the total for the whole Mediterranean theatre as well as unserviceable machines. According to the British Admiralty, there were 85 aircraft on Sicily alone on the 10th of August; and a further 64 undergoing repair.

The main strikes were carefully planned for the 12th of August when the convoy would be passing between the southern-most end of Sardinia and the approaches of Sicily, and when it would still be beyond fighter cover from Malta.

The first, shortly after 9 a.m., was to be made by

twenty Junkers 88s and was timed to coincide with
submarine attacks.

At midday, a big effort was to be made from the
Sardinian airfields with more than seventy aircraft
heavily escorted by fighters. It was to combine all
known forms of air attack with the addition of an Italian
secret weapon which was being used for the first time.
While eighteen fighter and dive-bombers made low-level
attacks, ten Savoia 79 Italian bombers were to drop
'Motobomba FFs' some hundreds of yards ahead of the
British force. The 'Motobomba FF' was a species of
circling torpedo or mobile mine attached to a parachute.
When it touched the water, a pressure mechanism
started an electrically-operated propeller which drove
the mine in wide circles.

These 'Motobombas' and the low level attacks were
designed to dislocate the formation of the British force
and draw their anti-aircraft fire, opening up the ships to
the torpedo attack which was to follow within five
minutes.

These torpedo attacks by forty-two bombers were to
be launched from ahead and on either side of the convoy,
so that whichever way the British ships turned to 'comb'
(that is turning towards the direction of the attack, to
present a smaller target to the torpedoes) one group of
bombers would be presented with the full length of the
ships.

The next stage of the strike was to consist of shallow
dive-bombing by German aircraft, after which two
Italian Reggione 2001s were to attack one of the aircraft
carriers with two heavy anti-personnel bombs. It was
hoped that these bombers, which resembled Hurricanes,
would be able to approach the carrier without being
fired upon and that the anti-personnel bombs with their
high fragmentation would severely damage the aircraft
and men crowding the flight deck during the latter part
of an action.

Another secret weapon, a glider bomb launched from

a special aircraft and remotely controlled by radio, was also to have been used against another carrier, but this device developed defects and could not be employed.

The Axis plan for this final air attack on the 12th was conceived so as to make the maximum use of Mediterranean dusk conditions. Planned for 6.30, a quarter of an hour after sunset, when the convoy would be bearing towards the south-east to round Cape Bon, this main strike was to be developed from ahead, out of the darkened eastern sky. While the British gunners would be hampered by the gathering darkness in this direction, the Axis pilots would see the convoy clearly silhouetted against the sunset glow in the west. Formation leaders had orders to delay their attack until these conditions gave them the maximum advantage.

The force allotted to this was the biggest to be thrown against the convoy, numbering 100 aircraft, German Junkers 87 dive-bombers and Junkers 88 bombers and Italian Savoia 79 torpedo aircraft.

The attack was to open with dive-bombing from ahead and astern of the convoy in an attempt to scatter the ships and absorb the attention of the gunners. Meanwhile, the torpedo aircraft were to deliver an attack out of the dark side of the sky, followed by shallow dive-bombing by the main force of bombers. Heavy fighter cover was to be provided, although the Axis planners hoped that by dusk most of the fleet fighters would have landed on the British carriers. As in the midday sortie, individual attacks with anti-personnel bombs were to be made on these ships.

In theory, by dawn on the 13th of August, a scattered, thinned-out convoy, perforce deserted by their battleships and heavy units, would lie at the mercy of the Italian fleet. With four Italian battleships and at least two cruiser squadrons at their disposal, the Axis seemed to possess a commanding position from which no element of the convoy could escape.

The planning of this naval action, however, had to be

subject to the Italian shortage of oil. This lack of oil for their ships may have been one of the minor reasons behind the abandonment of operation 'Hercules'. Indeed, for many months, the shortage and the German inability to make it good effectively had exercised restraint on Italian naval operations, so that it had seldom been possible for them to put to sea with their entire fleet.

In January 1942, after continued appeals from the Italians, the German Supreme Command wrote to Admiral Weichold: 'Italy must realize that she is continually putting forward requirements for fuel oil which cannot be met until new sources of supply are captured.'

Since then, opposing two convoys had cost the Italian fleet 15,000 tons of oil, and the German admiral had advised his superiors that their ally's oil stocks were almost exhausted.

So it was that when the Italians came to plan the attack on 'Operation Pedestal' they had fuel sufficient for one battleship but only for two at a pinch. They came to the conclusion that to put out against the main British force with two battleships would be an ineffectual gesture in the face of so powerful an enemy.

This lack of the means to sail with heavy elements created great anxiety among the Axis planners lest the British should try to run through a supporting convoy from Alexandria, and it seems that had they done so it might have met with even greater success than 'Pedestal', for the Italians had no means of blocking it effectively. The oil situation was, however, not known to the British.

Under the circumstances the Italians decided to sail with two cruiser divisions, the Third and Seventh, with the object of intercepting the convoy at dawn south of Pantelleria. Consisting of the heavy cruisers *Gorizia*, *Bolzano* and *Trieste*, armed with heavy modern 8-inch main armament, the cruisers *Montecuccoli*, *Attendolo* and *Eugenio*, mounting 6-inch guns and an escort of eleven destroyers, this fleet was in a position to achieve a notable success for they outgunned, outnumbered and had the speed to outmanœuvre the British force, once the main fleet had turned back at the 'Narrows'.

As soon as the convoy was reported, the two cruiser divisions with their escorting destroyers sailed from the ports of Cagliari, Messina and Naples, with orders to rendezvous 100 miles north of Marittimo.

While the convoy was steaming on towards the 'Narrows' and towards the combination of sea and air attack which had been prepared for it, Kapitanleutnant Helmut Rosenbaum, commander of the German submarine, U.73, was congratulating himself on having travelled from Spezia to his patrol position off Algiers without being spotted by British aircraft. On his previous voyage, ferrying supplies to Tobruk, his 500-ton U-boat had been caught in shallow water by the RAF Hudsons and had its stern completely shattered by a bomb. Without wireless, leaking badly and forced to remain on the surface, he had succeeded in limping 1,200 miles back to port without being caught by the British anti-submarine patrols. After that miracle it seemed that his luck still held.

His departure had scarcely been auspicious. News of the British convoy had forced him to put to sea with a leaking exhaust cut-out, an unserviceable direction-finding aerial, leaks in the main bilge pump and periscope and a slipping clutch on the main drive of the diesel engines. Now more than half his crew were ill with enteritis and unfit, in his opinion, for the perilous duty of breaking through the convoy screen and torpedo-ing an aircraft-carrier, one of the most heavily protected units of the fleet. If only his luck would hold . . . it was his eighth patrol and at the end of it he was due for leave and the command of a new pocket submarine flotilla in the comparatively safe waters of the Black Sea.

They were lying peacefully at a depth of 100 feet. It was the morning of the 11th of August. Suddenly a voice cut into the low humming of the dynamos: 'Propeller noises approaching from the westward.'

Immediately, the narrow confines of the U-boat became a scene of feverish activity. Course was changed and tanks blown until U.73 reached periscope depth heading towards the sounds they had picked up on the hydrophone listening device.

'Up periscope.' Rosenbaum, his eyes pressed firmly to a small, round window on the upper world, swept the sea for a sight of the enemy. Almost immediately he picked up the masts of a destroyer about three miles away on the starboard bow. At the same moment an aircraft-carrier appeared looking like 'a giant matchbox floating on a pond'. The commander methodically counted five destroyers and other smaller ships circling round her. The carrier was travelling at about twelve knots, zigzagging with almost right-angled turns and varying in range from the U-boat between three and five miles.

Menacing propeller noises approached and a destroyer loomed in the periscope view. Quickly he took the U.73 down to 100 feet. Then he ordered full speed, closing the aircraft-carrier on an almost parallel course, and returned to periscope depth.

The aircraft-carrier was last in the starboard line of the convoy escort and he identified it as *Eagle*. There were seven destroyers between him and his prey now. A dangerous moment was approaching when he would have to dive under this screen. He took another quick look and dived. Overhead the thud of propellers could be heard and he knew that the eerie bleep-bleep of the British Asdic sets would be sending out fingers of sound which could locate the submarine as they rebounded from its steel hull. The next sound was most likely to be the crash of depth-charges exploding round him, the scream of the breaking hull and the inrushing of black waters.

Somehow they escaped detection. Perhaps it was one

of those density layers of cold water above him which
abound in the Mediterranean and which would have
shielded him from the Asdic's probe. Another quick
look through the periscope and he was breaking through
between the third and fourth destroyer with less than
400 yards to spare on either side. Still the U.73 was
undetected.

Now he was making his attack run, reading off bearings as he watched through the periscope. He held his
fire while the convoy passed through the circle of sea
and air which his periscope covered. Then the carrier
loomed, filling all his vision. He turned slightly to port
holding the great ship within the crossed wires of the
sight. 'Fire.' With shudders and sudden air pressure in
the submarine, a salvo of 4 torpedoes, set to run 20 feet
below the surface at a range of 500 yards, were on their
way.

Rosenbaum gave the order to dive deeply. As they
were diving to avoid the retribution which was sure to
follow, they heard four muffled explosions, then a
strange cracking, creaking sound and a drawn-out rending groan.

CHAPTER EIGHT

For What We Are About to Receive

Senior Officer Force F to Admiralty:
HMS EAGLE SUNK STOP TORPEDOED BY
SUBMARINE POSITION 038 DEGREES 05 MINUTES
NORTH 003 DEGREES 02 MINUTES EAST STOP 11/8/42
END MESSAGE

One after another, at two-second intervals, great plumes of brown water had reared up, to three times the height of *Eagle*'s mainmast, as the salvo of four torpedoes exploded along her port side.

With clouds of black smoke wreathing behind her she dragged quickly to a stop, and as she slowed she listed progressively farther and farther.

Within three minutes the whole of her deck could be seen tilted at an angle of almost forty-five degrees and toy-like aircraft began to slide and fall from her, splashing into the sea. The tiny figures of men could be seen clambering, slipping and sliding down the increasing angle of her decks and now half-exposed bottom.

The destroyers *Lookout* and *Laforey* sped towards her at thirty-one knots in a lather of white water, and the tug *Jaunty* bore down, her crew making ready towing gear.

With sirens roaring, fleet and convoy turned sharply to protect themselves.

Away to the left of the sinking ship, the cruiser *Charybdis* hit back. Zigzagging over the calm waters she dropped pattern after pattern of depth-charges, the sea boiling up behind her in great geysers of white water at half-minute intervals.

But nothing could be done to aid the stricken aircraft-carrier. With slow dignity the veteran warrior of a dozen Mediterranean battles rolled gently on to her side. The crackle of exploding bulkheads and tearing metal came faintly across the blue sea and then she was gone in a swirl of debris and troubled water. She had sunk in less than eight minutes, and now the sea had a film of dark oil on it speckled with the black heads of her crew, the grey life-saving rafts and the boats from the destroyers which were picking up survivors.

Of her company of 1,160, 900 were saved including her commander, Captain L. D. Mackintosh. A patrol of four of her aircraft, in the air at the time, landed on other carriers, but twenty-five per cent of the fleet's air cover had been lost.

Northward, a distant tower of cumulus cloud marked the place where the Balearic island of Majorca lay below the horizon and a deepening of the haze southward showed that here lay the low line of the North African coast and the hostile Vichy French port of Algiers. Malta still lay 550 miles distant. The sirens boomed again and the convoy, precise as guardsmen on parade, zigzagged ninety degrees to port, away from *Eagle*'s grave.

Anxious eyes again scanned the empty sea, searching for the white ribbons of torpedo tracks or the momentary feather of a periscope. Others swept the hot, hazy sky, for the hum of shadowing enemy aircraft had been with them for five hours despite everything fighters flown from the fleet carriers *Victorious*, *Indomitable* and *Eagle* had done to hound the snoopers.

Up to that moment 'Pedestal's' passage had been almost uneventful. At first it had seemed that complete surprise had been gained.

That morning, the fog in which they had passed through the Straits, had dispersed, the brassy sun caused the slight haze to dance and a hot east wind stippled the dark blue waters with flecks of white. The visibility was alarmingly good.

—

At 8.15 the corvette *Coltsfoot* had reported two torpedoes porpoising harmlessly. They had been fired by the Italian submarine *Uarsceik*, which had first reported the presence of the convoy in the Mediterranean. Fifteen minutes later, radar located the first of the snooping aircraft. Carrier-borne Hurricanes and Fulmars made five interceptions, shooting down one Junkers 88 for the loss of two of our fighters.

Admiral Syfret knew for certain that his force was discovered at 10.55 a.m. when Mussolini's Rome radio broadcast details of it to all Italian stations and units.

Then out of the sea's depth had come the salvo which had sunk *Eagle*.

The sun moved overhead, dazzling the watchers, and the convoy drove on towards Malta at fifteen knots, cutting an intricate pattern of varied zigzags.

'For what we are about to receive . . .' murmured a Chief Yeoman aboard the flagship, unconsciously repeating the irreverent saying of seamen about to stand an enemy broadside in Nelson's time.

At 2.20 p.m. the men watching the crotchets of light on the radar screen saw them suddenly lengthen in a compact group on the southward side of their graticules.

In every ship the warning was broadcast: 'Enemy aircraft approaching from the starboard beam.'

Gun mountings swung in unison as the barrels of the anti-aircraft batteries groped skywards. The gunners adjusted their tin helmets and waited tensely, fingering the triggers. Perhaps this was 'it'.

Presently the thin drone of engines could be heard. They seemed directly overhead. With a rending crack, the primary anti-aircraft armament of *Nelson* and *Rodney* opened up, firing a controlled barrage. Again and again the guns' flashes sparkled even in the bright daylight and the crackle of the reports smote the onlookers with physical force.

Overhead, stars of black shell-burst dotted the sky

very high up. Except those serving the heaviest armament the gunners held their fire, for no aircraft was
visible. Evidently, the enemy was carrying out a photographic reconnaissance. Then the battleships fell silent
and the bumbling drone drew away northwards.

Later that afternoon Admiral Syfret received the welcome signal that 'Operation Bellows' had succeeded.
Thirty-six Spitfires had landed in Malta.

The flying off of these aircraft from *Furious* had been
interrupted by the sinking of *Eagle*. Then the remainder
of the Spitfires had been launched. One, which developed engine trouble, landed on *Indomitable*.

Furious then stood back to Gibraltar with her escort
and success remained with her. *Wolverine*, one of her
screen of destroyers, rammed and sank the Italian submarine *Dagabur* on the way.

The afternoon waned away and the blue of the waters
deepened. The sun approached the sea, a red ball in a
haze of violet and gold. It was almost too late for an air
attack.

> Vice-Admiral Commanding North Atlantic to
> Senior Officer, Force F:
> INTERCEPTED ENEMY WIRELESS TRAFFIC INDICATES
> THAT AIRCRAFT MAY ATTACK CONVOY AT DUSK
> MESSAGE ENDS

Admiral Syfret ordered the fleet to take up action
stations again and the destroyers fanned away from the
convoy. Then radar detected the new raid approaching.

The carriers, only two of them now, belched smoke
and turned into the wind, racing away from the convoy
at full speed to fly off their protecting aircraft. The gnat-
like formations of fighters formed up and climbed away,
glinting in the setting sun.

Then the leading destroyer on the port side of the
convoy was firing with everything she had got. Cruisers,

—

then the battleships, joined in with an inferno of shock and sound.

The convoy could see them coming now – thirty-six little cruciform shapes, Junkers 88s and Heinkel 111s with torpedoes, diving from 5,000 feet out of the blackness of approaching night. Tracers streaked. Red, green and gold, they made an umbrella of light in the dusk, picked out with the tinsel of scores of bursting shells.

Above the roar of the gunnery, the whine of aero engines rose to a tortured scream. The aircraft grew bigger and began to pull out of their dives.

A half-heard cheer sounded. A Junkers 88 came spinning down to port with both wings on fire. It had been hit by the tug *Jaunty*. Another Junkers, streaming black smoke, flattened as the automatic pull-out came into action, and crashed belly first in a flurry of spray.

Columns of sea shot into the air as the bombs landed with the heavy drumming of underwater explosions. Aircraft howled overhead, jinking and turning, followed by the turning, spitting barrels of the guns.

As the torpedo bombers turned away short of the convoy, the water creamed with torpedo tracks and the warning roar of the sirens added to the din as the warships heeled over in emergency turns followed by the convoy.

The last of the enemy aircraft skimmed overhead, living miraculously in a hail of crossfire, till a red glow lit the fuselage, and then it spun away in the gathering darkness flaming like a misdirected rocket.

Suddenly the guns stopped. The silence was almost painful. It was night now. Somehow fleet and convoy had escaped damage. The gunners removed their tin hats, blew out their cheeks and wiped the sweat from their eyes. Then they moved, stretching stiffly. The fight was over for the present.

It was a blessedly peaceful night. The hot decks cooled and while the off-duty men of the fleet and convoy slept, Beaufighters and Liberators of the RAF from Malta bombed and straffed the enemy aircraft at their aerodromes.

As a turquoise glow began to appear in the east, radar warned that the enemy snooping aircraft were about again and the admiral ordered the guns to a first degree of readiness.

The day began with a victory for the Fleet Air Arm.

As the convoy moved into defensive positions again and as the men snatched a hasty breakfast at action stations, a squadron of twelve fighters took off from the carrier's decks, the sun touching their wings with golden fire as they turned.

At five past nine, the deep drone of twin-engined enemy bombers could be heard. Soon after they came into view, flying very high in close formation. The British fighters were there too, up sun of the enemy, and were diving now in line astern weaving through the enemy's ranks. The high whine of engines was followed by the distant crackle of machine-guns.

Lieutenant R. H. P. Carver, flying a Hurricane of 885 Squadron, drove into the enemy formation and attacked a Junkers 88 from astern firing burst after burst into it. It turned and dived away with its port engine smoking. The lieutenant turned his attention to another 88 and carried out a stern attack, then diving, turning and climbing he attacked it again and again from the beam. It turned over and crashed into the sea.

The other fighters, too, were attacking the formation. Two more Junkers 88s came spinning down, while another turned back towards Italy, one engine smoking. Already the enemy had begun to break up, so that when the bombs fell they were widely scattered and fell harmlessly into the sea.

Not long after the fighters were landing on the carriers again, the pilots jubilant because they had destroyed eight enemy aircraft for certain and probably three others.

—

Other convoy hunters were early astir. Fifteen minutes after the aircraft had been driven off, *Fury*, on the starboard wing of the convoy, confirmed by Asdic contact the presence of an enemy submarine. *Fury* and *Laforey* attacked, dropping pattern after pattern of depth-charges.

Two hours passed, punctuated by spasmodic firing from the screen ships as snooping aircraft ventured too near and by the occasional depth-charging of submarine contacts by the destroyers.

Then, at 11.35 a.m., the German U.205 made a determined attempt to break through the destroyer screen and attack the merchantmen.

Destroyer *Pathfinder*, steaming on the port bow of the convoy, reported the contact first and, assisted by *Zetland*, went in to the attack. Down the side of the convoy they hunted the submarine, forcing her to dive deeply, jinking desperately this way and that to avoid the underwater explosions.

Thus far no casualties had been suffered except *Eagle*, and as Admiral Burrough forecast, the shooting season had opened well; but while these attacks were being countered another was developing. At noon, another air-raid was reported coming in from ahead of the convoy. The distant smoke of falling aircraft was seen, then the destroyer *Ashanti* sighted the enemy hotly engaged by fleet fighters.

This was the major effort from the Sardinia airfields, but the first wave of ten Italian torpedo bombers, harried by the fighters, and daunted by the terrific barrage put up by the fleet, which included *Rodney*'s 16-inch armament used for the first time against aircraft, failed to press home their attack.

Ahead of the convoy black canisters on parachutes could be seen falling. Some of them appeared to be exploding in the water. An officer in *Nelson* made a note in the action diary on the first use of an Italian secret weapon. 'Black canisters dropped. Probably circling torpedoes.'

To avoid them fleet and convoy heeled in a ninety degree emergency turn, faultlessly carried out despite dive-bombing and machine-gunning from eight fighter-bombers.

As they turned, forty-one torpedo-bombers could be seen diving in from the port bow followed by another twenty-one on the starboard. The emergency turn had exposed the full length of the ships in the fleet and convoy to at least one group of bombers.

Up came the barrage again, black and crackling in the path of the torpedo-bombers, and another emergency turn was begun. The shooting was fast and accurate and it defeated this attack too. The Italian bombers turned away dropping their torpedoes 8000 yards short, well out of range of the convoy.

Only the screen destroyers on either side were in any danger, particularly those on the port side, and they were twisting and turning as the torpedoes passed close down their sides.

Then, with the scream of dive-brakes, twenty black German Junkers 87s fell upon the British ships. Bombs whistled down and towering columns of water sprang up beside *Nelson*. The battleship rocked as they exploded not far from her keel, and *Rodney* and the cruiser *Cairo* were also narrowly missed. This time the gunners failed to protect the convoy completely.

> *MV Deucalion* to Senior Officer F Force:
> NEAR MISSED BY BOMBS STOP PLATES BUCKLED
> UNDER STRAIN STOP NUMBER ONE HOLD HALF FILLED
> WITH WATER STOP NUMBER TWO HOLD COMPLETELY
> FLOODED MESSAGE ENDS

Deucalion, leading the port wing column of the convoy, rolled almost on her beam-ends as three bombs exploded alongside sending cascades of water crashing down on her foredeck. Destroyer *Bramham* sped to the merchantman's assistance. Slowly the injured ship slipped astern of the convoy, the crew working to shore up straining bulkheads, with the destroyer standing by. Then she began to steam slowly towards the African coast.

As the last of the dive-bombers was retreating, two aircraft approached Rear-Admiral Lyster's flagship, *Victorious*, and no one fired on them because they looked like Hurricanes. In the admiral's own words it seemed as though they were going to land on the carrier. Then they opened their throttles and two bombs dropped. The two pilots of these Italian Reggione fighter-bombers were less fortunate than their daring warranted, for the one bomb which hit the carrier's flight-deck amidships broke up without exploding.

The gunners now had time to wipe their blackened faces again. Aboard the cruiser *Nigeria* the ship's cat came out of a hiding-place behind the main armament and fed her three kittens in the hot sun.

Fighters had destroyed nine of the enemy aircraft and the ships had shot down two, but there was no rest for the destroyers of the screen, at least; for the following two hours brought innumerable reports of submarine sightings and Asdic contacts. In a brief exchange of signals Rear-Admiral Burrough suggested dropping a depth-charge every half-hour on either side of the convoy to 'discourage' the hovering U-boats, and Admiral Syfret at once made this suggestion an order.

Another message came in later that afternoon. *Bramham* reported that the fight to save *Deucalion* had failed. After two further air attacks, an aerial torpedo had hit the merchant vessel amidships and she had caught fire and blown up.

At 4.16 p.m., *Pathfinder*'s brilliant team of Asdic operators again reported a submarine working into an

attacking position ahead of the convoy. The destroyer
dashed in to counter it and two patterns of depth-charges
thundered down, apparently without result.

Twenty minutes later, the badly-shaken Italian submarine *Cobalto* bobbed suddenly to the surface close to
the destroyer *Ithuriel*. With forward armament quick-
firing, the destroyer bore down on the submarine and
her sharp bows crunched into it behind the conning
tower.

A boarding party leapt on to the outer casing of the
submarine to seize her crew and papers, but before they
could enter the conning tower she had already begun to
sink. The boarding party just had time to pull away
before she submerged for the last time. Three Italian
officers, one of them the captain, and thirty-eight enemy
ratings were captured. Meanwhile both *Tartar* and *Lookout* had sighted running torpedoes and carried out
attacks, hounding two more U-boats until they were
driven away to a safe distance. *Ithuriel*, with crushed
bows, limped back to Gibraltar.

So it was that, until the fleet and convoy reached to
within twenty miles of the Skerki channel, the combined enemy attacks were beaten. The destroyer screen,
thanks to the unwavering skill of radar and Asdic
operators, had looked deep into the sea, so that swift
counter-attacks had kept the U-boats at a safe distance.
Despite well co-ordinated air attacks, the gunners of
fleet and convoy had put up a terrific barrage, described
by all who saw it as the greatest and most lethal ever
experienced in the war at sea; and this, aided by the
determined onslaught of the fighter pilots, had either
resulted in wild and inaccurate bombing or had prevented the enemy aircraft from approaching to within
effective range.

For a full day, however, the British seamen had
endured continual attack from sea and air in the blister-
ing Mediterranean sun. The Axis forces were constantly

—

being thrown into the battle in fresh relays: there was no respite for the defenders, no opportunity to relax or sleep. Even when the attacks were not pressed home, even when they didn't materialize, Axis aircraft were continually threatening, hovering and circling round the convoy and were being picked up by radar. Consequently, the crews had to be always ready to repel an attack. With a few seconds' warning, or with none at all, the dive-bombers might come screaming down at them out of the sun, and then only rapid manœuvre and instantaneous barrage could save the ships from destruction. Whether by accident or design, the Axis tactics were wearing down the physical resistance of the defenders.

The gunners were half choked with cordite fumes, their senses dulled with the drumming of the barrage. The pilots of the Hurricanes and Fulmars were almost asleep in their cockpits. Deep down in the ships, the Asdic and radar operators knuckled their tired, red-rimmed eyes and steeled their ears to the crash of more close bombs clanging on the hulls.

At 6.30 p.m., when the fleet altered course to steer for the Skerki channel, it was evident that the enemy were building up for another great air attack. This was to come from the strongly held enemy airfields of Sicily, now dangerously close, and it was to consist of more than 100 bombers, strongly escorted by fighters.

For nearly an hour the enemy aircraft had been reported by radar and reconnaissance aircraft about twenty-five miles away from the convoy. Here they had been assembling, evidently to co-ordinate their attack.

Five minutes later thirteen Savoia torpedo bombers were seen diving in from ahead. Once again they were met by fierce barrage and once again they were compelled to drop their torpedoes 3,000 yards outside the screen.

Almost at the same moment, dive-bomber after dive-bomber screamed down upon the convoy from both astern and ahead.

In the pandemonium of bomb bursts, flying water and the roar of guns, the convoy began to turn to port to avoid more circling torpedoes. As they did so more torpedo-bombers could be seen attacking from the unprotected flank.

The exact sequence of the next few minutes is lost. With a brilliant flash, a torpedo hit the stern of the destroyer *Foresight*, lifting it almost out of the water, and she slewed to a stop, stern, rudder and screws all blown off. *Tartar* raced to her aid and, as both ships were rocked violently by bombs exploding nearby, a towline was passed. Both crews fought desperately to save her, but she was settling fast and, as she was without motive power, she had to be sunk later by her own forces as the fleet returned.

> *Indomitable* to Senior Officer F Force:
> SHIP HIT BY TWO OR THREE BOMBS DAMAGED BY
> NEAR MISSES STOP PETROL FIRES ON FLIGHT DECK
> MESSAGE ENDS

Though bombs were dropping among the merchant-men of the convoy and many were narrowly missed, the main enemy attack was being concentrated upon the carriers.

At two-second intervals, forty black Stuka bombers, their wing sirens screaming, peeled off from high above the fleet and dived at *Indomitable*. Columns of water shot into the air obscuring the carrier from the convoy. Then there was a great orange flash and billows of black smoke. Through it all the spark of the guns could be seen firing back continually.

As the curtain of water fell again, huge fires were burning fore and aft on the flight deck, but the guns were still firing.

The carrier turned down-wind to the westward to

minimize the fanning of the flames. The cruiser, *Charybdis* and her destroyers swept round after the carrier to form a protective screen against other attacks.

Though blazing petrol was swilling over the decks and cascading over the stern and beam in a fiery rain, *Lookout* ran alongside and men could be seen passing hoses on to the carrier's flight deck. Fire parties on the carrier had also been organized and as she disappeared astern of the convoy the fires were dying. This attack was carried out by the cream of Kesselring's Luftwaffe. Captain Frend of *Phoebe*, astern of *Indomitable*, reported that the enemy aircraft had dived through the thickest of barrages to press home the attack. They had scored a notable success. Had it not been for the twenty-two British fighters, all that could be mustered to repel the attack, casualties would probably have been much heavier. Though outnumbered by enemy fighters by two to one, the Hurricanes, Martlets and Fulmars had destroyed seven of the enemy. Two more had been shot down by the ships.

Admiral Syfret now had to make a vital decision. The capital ships with their escorts could not be risked in the 'Narrows'. Two hours previously he had signalled that Force Z, with the carriers, would turn back to Gibraltar at 7.15 p.m. leaving the convoy and its escort to proceed to Malta. Now it was 7 p.m. and the 'Narrows' were less than an hour's steaming away. Should he proceed farther with the convoy until night had removed the danger of air attacks, as Admiral Curteis had done in the June convoy, or should he retire at once, shielding the damaged carrier, the speed of which had been considerably reduced?

If he turned to the westward at once, the convoy would have to steam for two hours in daylight and twilight without the protection of the main fleet. Admiral Burrough had previously pointed out that these two hours were the most dangerous of all and the time at which the most successful air attacks were likely to be made. Admiral Burrough had also asked for some fighter protection at this period. This was now impossible. With the damage to *Indomitable* and the loss of *Eagle*, only about one-third of the fleet's protection remained. Moreover, the carriers had made a maximum effort in fighting off the last raid. In order to clear her decks *Victorious* had had to send off a patrol of four Fulmars which had been earmarked for the escort of Force X. These now had to be refuelled and rearmed and it would be impracticable to fly them off later to escort the convoy.

The admiral also had to consider the safety of the heavy units of the fleet under his command. He had already received warning to expect that a large force of enemy submarines would be waiting in the 'Narrows'. With no room to manœuvre, the battleships would be sitting targets there for the enemy torpedoes. Moreover, the strength of the recent attack gave him cause to hope that the enemy had expended, at least for the moment, most of their force, and it seemed unlikely that they could mount another large raid before night covered the convoy.

Perhaps the hardest decision Admiral Syfret had to take was whether or not to reinforce the convoy with more cruisers. In the mid-June convoy, inadequate cruiser strength with the escort, after the fleet had turned back, had contributed to the loss of all but two of the merchantmen. Signals already received from the RAF indicated that the Italian fleet might be at sea, although this report was not yet confirmed, and it was possible that early next morning Admiral Burrough's force would be beset not only by the enemy bombers but by a superior force of enemy ships as well. At the same time the admiral had to consider the safety of his own fleet and, in particular, *Indomitable*, now crippled and making not much more than thirteen knots. If he had to escort the carrier back to Gibraltar at slow speed, he would need every cruiser he had to supply anti-aircraft cover.

—

The admiral weighed all these considerations, then made his decision. At 7 p.m., fifteen minutes before he had previously intended to leave Force X, he signalled a heartfelt 'Godspeed' to Admiral Burrough, and orders were given to Force Z to retire to the westward.

The battleships gathered speed, then, heeling over, turned towards Gibraltar while their screen of cruisers and destroyers closed in upon them, and they were soon disappearing into the sunset.

The convoy, shaken but intact except for *Deucalion*, plodded stubbornly towards Malta and the oncoming night.

CHAPTER NINE

Disaster in the Narrows

Axum to CSC
SALVO SIX TORPEDOES FIRED AT CONVOY POSITION
037 DEGREES 40 MINUTES NORTH 010 DEGREES 05
MINUTES EAST AT 1956 HOURS STOP TWO CRUISERS
AND ONE MERCHANT SHIP BELIEVED SUNK END
MESSAGE

Kenya to Admiralty:
FORCE X POSITION AT 2030 37 DEGREES 40 MINUTES
NORTH 10 DEGREES 06 MINUTES EAST STOP NIGERIA
AND CAIRO TORPEDOED STOP CONVOY PROCEEDING
MALTA STOP VICE-ADMIRAL MALTA PLEASE ARRANGE
FIGHTER DIRECTION END MESSAGE

Captain Mason, tin hat tilted backwards, peered into the dusk from *Ohio*'s bridge. He turned to the naval liaison officer, Lieutenant Denys Barton.

'I think there are some more Jerry aircraft coming. Listen,' he said. The crew of *Ohio* already felt that their ship, clearly recognizable as a tanker, with the funnel so far aft, had been singled out as a target by the German aircraft.

So far, however, they had received no more than a wetting from near misses. The cargo upon which the future of Malta depended was intact.

The convoy was now entering the 'Narrows', and the merchant ships had slowed down to form from four into two lines.

Mason and Barton, and on the right wing of the bridge First Officer Gray and Stephen the Third, could see the

cruisers moving up to their stations ahead of the convoy
and destroyers forming screen in front of the cruisers.

'It's getting dark,' said Mason. 'I shouldn't be surprised
if . . .'

A bright flash lit up the flagship *Nigeria*. Flames and
smoke billowed from below the port side of her bridge.
Then the force of an explosion slapped into their faces.
The damaged ship slewed to starboard and began to list
farther and farther until it seemed she must capsize.
There was another flash and a huge geyser of water
spread up at the stern of *Cairo* just ahead of them. Huge
chunks of iron plate were hurled into the air.

'Hold on to your hats,' shouted Stephen. 'If there's
another torpedo in that salvo, we've . . .'

A roar, almost soundless in its immensity, knocked
them all flat on the deck. Pieces of hot metal and deluges
of water rained down round them.

Instinctively Mason crawled towards the chart-room
and collided at the door with Stephen.

'What's happened?' he gasped.

Fire above them was making a new daylight. Mason
jumped to his feet. 'We've hit a mine or something.
Come on.' All four officers ran towards the bridge ladder
and hesitated. Behind them, from the amidships section,
a huge pillar of flame leapt high into the air above mast
height, sighing and howling.

Captain Mason turned and scanned the sea ahead
quickly. He saw that the convoy, disorganized by the
stricken cruisers which were charging across its route,
was scattering in all directions. *Ohio*, too, seemed to be
out of control. He grabbed the engine-room telegraph:
'Shut down and come up,' he ordered. 'Get the deck
water lines on. We're on fire.'

This was probably the end. Once hit and on fire a
tanker stood little chance.

As Mason slid down the bridge ladder, a flight of
hostile aircraft screamed by at almost deck level and
bombs thundered into the water. Another close one. A

boat was being launched aft, but the guns were still
firing. The gunners seemed to be ignoring the flames
altogether. Other men were running towards the boats.
Two were already in one. The flames seemed to die a
little. Perhaps they could save her yet, but would the
men rally?

'Come out of that boat, Ginger,' the captain shouted.
'You're not getting among those Algerian women yet.'

The men in the boat turned, looked at him for a
moment, then made fast the falls. Mason realized that
there would be no panic. He could hear them laughing.

'Come on. Let's get that fire out,' he ordered and
seized a fire-extinguisher. They streamed along the
twisted cat-walks shielding their faces from the heat
with their free arms.

The heat was intense, but twenty men were already
fighting the fire at close quarters. The guns went on
firing. Another stick of bombs crashed into the sea,
sending water cascading all over the deck.

'They'll put the fire out if they're not careful,' some-
body panted.

Lighted kerosene was bubbling up from the fractured
tanks. Little gouts of flame spattered the deck to a
distance of thirty yards from the blaze.

The chief steward, Meeks, was beating them out with
his cap methodically. 'Like swatting flies,' he said later.
He had been one of the first on the scene, and had found
his second steward, a green first-voyager whom he had
had to chivvy remorselessly during the journey, standing
virtually on top of the seat of the explosion. The boy
was covered in fuel oil and dazed but miraculously
preserved. 'I suppose you're going to blame me for this
as well,' he wailed.

'Of course I shall,' Meeks replied, 'so you'd better
come and help put it out.'

The flames dipped lower and then blazed up again.
There were cries for more extinguishers. The men made
another charge on the wall of heat.

Meanwhile, in *Nigeria* all the lights had gone out. The steering gear had jammed, causing her to circle out of control, and throughout the ship the roar of water pouring into her could be plainly heard.

The men began to clamber on deck ready to abandon ship. They found Admiral Burrough leaning calmly over the side of the bridge in the negligent attitude of a peacetime yachtsman on the Solent.

'Don't worry, she'll hold,' said the admiral casually. 'Let's have a cigarette.'

That settled it; the men ran to emergency stations. Under the orders of Captain Paton gallons of water were swiftly pumped into the starboard tanks and the heavy list was soon reduced to a gentle tilt. Other parties manned the emergency steering equipment and the cruiser was brought under control again.

The admiral unhurriedly transferred his flag to the destroyer *Ashanti*, and the damaged flagship was able to proceed at fourteen knots back toward Gibraltar.

Before he left *Nigeria*, Admiral Burrough shouted a last message to the ship's company: 'I hate leaving you like this, but my job is to go on and get that convoy to Malta. And I'm going to do it whatever happens.' The men wanted to go on. 'We'll all see it through,' they shouted. The admiral shook his head. 'No,' he said, 'your job is to stop here and get your own ship safely home.' They cheered him as he went over the side.

Cairo, however, was in a desperate situation, sinking fast, and it was plain that she could not outlast the night. Orders were given to take off her crew and sink her with gunfire.

On *Ohio* the fire was under control. A hail from the port side distracted Captain Mason's attention from the blaze. He saw that the destroyer *Ashanti*, now the flagship, was gliding alongside. Admiral Burrough leaned over the bridge.

'Are you all right?' he called.

Mason wiped the sweat from his eyes. 'Fine, thanks. We can attend to this.'

'Oh, good show. I'll have to be off now. Rather busy, you know,' said Burrough, and the destroyer raced away again.

The captain went back to the job in hand. The amidships pump-room door had been blown open by the explosion, and regardless of flying spatters of burning paraffin he and Pumpman Collins peered in.

'More extinguishers here,' the captain shouted. There was a rush of feet and the flames, fought from another quarter, began to die still further. Pumpman Collins paused for breath and glanced over at a merchant ship passing close to port (she was probably the American *Almeria Lykes*).

He nudged the Bofors gun-layer: 'Look at that.' A mine had caught on the cab of the bridge and was swinging gently on its parachute lines. A man was calmly sawing away at the silk strands with his clasp knife.

'If *that* mine goes up it'll blow his bloody tin hat off,' said Collins. The two men looked at each other and roared with laughter. The mine fell with a splash into the water and the man, leaning out over the side, watched it float astern. The fire in the pump-room was now almost out.

Mason shouted: 'Keep at it, men,' and after a quick look round returned to the bridge, ducking as another flight of Junkers 88s roared over, their bombs cascading the foredeck with water.

On the bridge he called the engine-room: 'How long before we can get under way?' he asked.

Chief Engineer Jimmy Wyld had been watching the steam-gauge in the engine-room when the torpedo had struck. In the darkness he had struggled on deck to help fight the flames and then, returning to the engine-room, found that Higgins, the electrician, had restored the electric circuit.

"*Ohio*, famous, fabulous, never to be forgotten"

Admiral Burrough wishing Captain Mason of *Ohio* good luck, after the
Convoy Conference

Above, H.M.S. *Nigeria*; *below*, H.M.S. *Ashanti*; *bottom left*, Rear-Admiral Sir Harold Burrough; *bottom right*, Vice-Admiral Sir Neville Syfret

Italian torpedo bomber making its run over a ship in convoy

H.M.S. *Bramham*

Above, Brisbane Star; *below,* Melbourne Star; *bottom,* H.M.S. Ledbury

The survivors arrive in Valetta: *above, Rochester Castle*; *below, Port Chalmers*

Below, Ohio, supported by H.M.S. *Penn* and H.M.S. *Bramham,* limping towards Malta

The merchantman *Dorset* under attack

Italian reconnaissance photograph of S.S. *Waimarama* burning after dive
bombing

Ohio's deck above the torpedo hole

Triumph. Still just afloat, *Ohio* enters Grand Harbour

Captain Dudley Mason recovering in hospital. He was later awarded the George Cross

On the 19th September, 1946, the hulk of the *Ohio* was towed out to sea and sunk by gunfire

Having made an examination of the engines, he was able to tell the captain: 'We've a fairly clean bill of health here. The fires were blown out but we'll have the engines going within half an hour. How's the ship?'

Mason's voice crackled back: 'Seaworthy, I think. You'd better come up and we'll have a proper look.'

On the bridge, the second officer pointed towards the binnacle. 'Gyro's gone, sir.' Gray, the chief officer, added: 'Steering gear, too; we'll have to use the emergency gear.' Wyld joined the group.

'How are the phone lines?' he asked.

'We've still got one line to the after steering position,' Gray volunteered.

The captain nodded. 'We'll have to steer from aft. You take over there, Gray. I'll con her from here by phone.' Then, as an afterthought, 'Thank God for an American ship. Plenty of telephone lines.'

Gray hurried aft. Together the captain and the chief engineer surveyed the damage. A hole, twenty-four feet by twenty-seven feet, had been torn in the port side of the amidships pump-room. The blast had also blown another smaller hole in the starboard side and the compartment was flooded. There were jagged tears in the bulkheads and kerosene was bubbling from adjoining tanks, seeping in a film out through the holes in the hull. The deck had been broken open, so that one could look down between the tongues of torn plates right into the vitals of the ship. From beam to beam the deck was buckled but the ship held together.

Wyld grunted: 'That's welding. Rivets would never have stood it.'

The captain nodded and said: 'Let's hope she goes on holding. Take it slowly when you open up or she'll break her back.' Wyld went below to start the engines.

A new problem awaited Mason on the bridge. The gyro compass was broken and the magnetic compass seemed to have been blasted off its bearings. In the darkness, and unsure of their position, there seemed no way of steering a course to Malta.

As soon as *Nigeria* had been torpedoed, Captain A. S. Russell of *Kenya*, not knowing what had happened to Admiral Burrough, took over command of the convoy. He immediately made two emergency alterations of course to starboard by siren, followed by a general signal for increase of speed.

Some of the ships obeyed the orders and some did not. Before many minutes passed the merchantmen were in a heterogeneous mess, 'all scrummed up', as one liaison officer described it, and despite *Kenya*'s efforts to lead them back into the original course, all formation was lost.

Three destroyers, *Bicester*, *Wilton* and *Derwent*, were escorting *Nigeria* back to Gibraltar; and many of the remaining ten destroyers were standing by damaged ships and out of touch with *Kenya*.

In this scattered and disorganized condition, screen and convoy were in no shape to resist the heavy air attack which now fell upon them.

At 8.35 p.m. just after the sun had gone down, twenty German Junkers 88s came roaring in for a mast-high bombing attack.

The convoy fought back as best it could. Aboard the American *Almeria Lykes*, they made some good shooting and two of the enemy planes, caught in the merchantman's vicious barrage, crashed into the sea.

As the first attack waned, they changed the barrel of their Bofors gun. The other had been worn smooth by the continual firing.

One twenty-year-old American seaman, chewing gum imperturbably behind the bridge-wing Oerlikon, shouted to another crew man: 'Get a bucket of water, bud, this barrel's melting and there's more of the bastards coming.'

Twenty aircraft were diving in with torpedoes. This time with the convoy straggling over some miles of the

Mediterranean, there could be no concerted emergency turn, no controlled barrage.

From astern of them, Admiral Burrough ordered his flagship *Ashanti* and the destroyer *Penn*, which had been rounding up stragglers, to make smoke in the rear of the merchantmen to prevent their silhouettes from showing up in the dusk glow to the west, but it was too late.

One torpedo blew a great hole in the bows of *Brisbane Star* and the merchantman, out of control, careered across the path of the convoy.

To avoid being rammed, *Empire Hope* stopped her engines, and, while in this position, three dive-bombers delivered an attack on her. The second stick obtained a direct hit on hatch No. 4 and the three other bombs dropped close. The cased aviation petrol caught fire at once and within a moment she was burning fiercely. With blazing petrol spreading swiftly over the sea, the crew abandoned ship. From *Brisbane Star* they could hear the screams of badly-burnt men as the boats pulled away.

The bombers delivered attack after attack. The water round the ships boiled and seethed with exploding bombs. Then, with a crash which could be heard plainly on the Tunisian coast, *Clan Ferguson*, hit by a stick of bombs, blew up. An orange mushroom of flame, black smoke and flying debris gushed from her amidships. Within a few minutes nothing was left but a great blazing pyre of petrol on the surface of the sea. The Italian submarine *Alagi* later picked up fifty-three of the surviving members of her crew.

The convoy was now scattered over an area of twenty miles, lit eerily by the two flaming patches which were all that remained of *Empire Hope* and *Clan Ferguson*.

Force X had lost the protection of two of its cruisers, *Nigeria* and *Cairo*, and of the fourteen merchantmen eleven only remained, and two of them, *Ohio* and

Brisbane Star, lay astern, stopped and seriously damaged.

Of the screen, Admiral Burrough now had only the two cruisers, *Kenya* and *Manchester*, and ten destroyers.

It was at this critical juncture, with the convoy scattered and hard hit that the admiral received a signal informing him that the Italian fleet was at sea. Definite sighting reports from the RAF at Malta informed him that three heavy and three light cruisers with a destroyer screen were making south.

It meant that at dawn he was likely to have to fight an action, outnumbered and outgunned, somewhere in the neighbourhood of Pantelleria with the enemy airfields only fifteen miles away.

CHAPTER TEN

E-boats Attack

I

As Admiral Burrough made his way at full speed towards the van of the scattered convoy, he knew that the situation was critical.

When Admiral Syfret, returning to Gibraltar, had learned of the loss of *Cairo* and the damage to *Nigeria*, he had immediately sent back the cruiser *Charybdis*, escorted by two destroyers, to join Force X and Admiral Burrough had received a signal to the effect that they would reach him just before dawn.

The Italian force, however, which he might expect to meet early next day, still greatly outnumbered and outgunned the ships he could bring to bear.

Moreover, they were now approaching the narrowest part of the Tunisian channel where both U-boats and E-boats would by lying in wait for them. What was more, the convoy had broken up and it would be next to impossible to gather it together during darkness.

Even among the warships themselves, muddle and uncertainty was rife. As the position stood at 9 p.m. on the 12th of August, Captain Russell in *Kenya*, not knowing where Admiral Burrough was, had signalled Force X that he had taken command.

When the admiral heard this, he called for full speed so as to reach the van of the convoy without delay. As *Ashanti* hurried through the dark, they had a very narrow shave. As the last of the torpedo-bombers carried out an attack, *Ashanti*'s captain saw a torpedo approaching his starboard bow, and, travelling at full speed, he ordered a maximum turn to starboard. *Ashanti* heeled over sharply, shuddering as she turned. For a tense moment it seemed that they must be hit, then the torpedo passed swiftly down the starboard side missing only by two feet.

As Admiral Burrough reached the head of the convoy, a brilliant flash followed by a loud report told him that more trouble had beset the convoy. This time it was not so serious as it might have been.

Lying in wait in the narrowest part of the Tunisian channel, the Italian submarine *Alagi* had fired four torpedoes at *Kenya*. At the moment the salvo was discharged, *Kenya*'s lookout spotted the submarine on the surface, and a turn was made at full helm towards her. One torpedo hit the forefoot, blowing off the stem from the waterline downwards. Due to the quick turn, the other torpedoes, which would probably have sunk her, passed, one under the bridge and two close to the stern.

After stopping for a moment to examine the damage, it was found that the cruiser could still proceed with a fair turn of speed, so she rejoined *Manchester* at the head of the convoy. Shortly afterwards Admiral Burrough took over effective command of the convoy again, or that part of it which still remained in sight, consisting of only three of the merchantmen.

Meanwhile the damaged *Brisbane Star* had been plodding on alone following a course round Cape Bon given her by Admiral Burrough.

Suddenly the shape of a warship loomed out of the night. They were about to signal her when she was recognized as an Italian, a cruiser, they thought. In fact it was a large Italian destroyer, *Malocello*, laying mines, but she did not attack the merchant ship for fear of giving her position away as she was laying mines in French territorial waters.

Later, while close in to the shore, Captain Riley had an amusing exchange of messages with the hostile Vichy French signals station in the Gulf of Hammamet.

Hammamet signalled them first: 'You should hoist your signal letters.'

Brisbane Star: 'Please excuse me.'

Hammamet: 'You should anchor.'

Brisbane Star: 'My anchors are fouled. I cannot anchor.'

Hammamet: 'You appear to be dragging your bow and stern anchors.'

Brisbane Star: 'I have no stern anchors.'

Hammamet: 'You should anchor immediately.'

Brisbane Star: 'I cannot anchor. My anchors are fouled.'

Hammamet: 'Do you require a salvage or rescue?'

Brisbane Star: 'No.'

Hammamet: 'It is not safe to go too fast.'

Brisbane Star then steamed off at her maximum five knots.

II

On board *Ohio*, steam had been raised and by 8.45 p.m. they were ready to get under way once more. After discussion with Lieutenant Barton, Mason decided that it would be best to steer for the coast and then to stop while making a more thorough examination of the damage. They also decided that it would probably be impracticable to rejoin the convoy and therefore determined to keep as long as possible in French territorial waters and then proceed independently to Malta.

The problem was how this was to be accomplished without any serviceable compasses. In the darkness on the starboard side lay the African coast. To port were mine-fields.

Mason and Barton did some quick navigational reckoning and fixed upon a star which they hoped would give them a rough course towards the Cani rocks. Captain Mason rang for slow speed and *Ohio* began to

move again. Despite the damage the crew of the tanker
had succeeded in improvising a workable means of
steering during the hour since the torpedo had struck.

The steering gear in the wheelhouse was not working,
but the rudder could be moved by operating the valve on
the steering engine at the after end of the poop. From
this position no one could see ahead nor could the
operator tell how far to move the rudder because the
funnel and the deck-house stood in the way. Gray and
Stephen were therefore sent to the poop to operate the
steering engine, keeping in touch with the bridge by the
one remaining telephone line.

From the bridge, Mason, Barton and McKilligan passed
back directions to the poop checking the turns made by
the ship on an electrically operated rudder indicator
which was still working. Barton, at the telephone, would
tell the chief officer, for instance to 'put some port
rudder on'. Barton then watched the rudder indicator
and the swing of the bows, judging when to put some
opposite rudder on to stop the ship swinging too far.
This elaborate method seldom worked accurately and
the ship proceeded on her way in a series of none too
gentle curves, but with practice they were soon making
good a fairly constant course.

Thus the direction of the ship was controlled from
two isolated islands connected only by a single telephone line.

On the 'after island' when the initial difficulties of
steering had been ironed out, Gray remembered that he
had a full gallon jar of rum down in his quarters. The jar
was fetched and a large tot served to all hands on the
poop. It seemed to help a lot.

Whether *Ohio* would have survived the navigational
dangers of the night with these makeshift methods, and
whether she would have lasted the next day, alone and
a tempting target for the enemy airmen, it is impossible
to say, though it seems doubtful. Help was, however,
close at hand. About an hour and a half after they got

under way again the profile of a *Hunt*-class destroyer loomed up out of the night and a British voice hailed them.

'You must steer 120° if you want to catch up with the convoy,' it said. 'Or do you want a tow?'

Mason went to the wing of the bridge: 'No, thank you, we're under our own steam, but we haven't got a compass. Can you lead us to the convoy?'

The destroyer was *Ledbury* (Lieutenant-Commander Roger Hill) which had been sent to round up stragglers.

Hill soon had a stern light rigged. Slowly he began to lead *Ohio* along the course previously taken by the remainder of the convoy.

The sea ahead was still lit by flaming petrol from two stricken merchantmen. On the bridge of *Ohio*, Mason suddenly realized that they must pass almost through one of the patches of flames. He seized the loudhailer: 'For God's sake keep clear of that. We're oozing paraffin,' he shouted, and the destroyer sheered sharply to port.

Ohio steamed on following the shielded blue light in *Ledbury*'s stern. They were now inside the mine-fields of the 'Narrows', and the gleam of Cape Bon lighthouse stood abeam and began to slide astern. Slowly the tanker's speed began to increase, first to ten knots then to twelve, finally she was making a good sixteen knots, though she had to carry a continuous five degrees of starboard helm because of the great rent in her port side.

Mason made frequent examinations of the shattered deck. The ship creaked and groaned and the scraping of jagged metal could be heard somewhere down in the hold as the increased speed put greater strain upon the damaged section. The ship still held together, however. The buckling across the deck had not visibly increased, so they carried on and hoped for the best.

There was now time for a roll-call to be held and it showed that four men were missing, and No. 5 boat was trailing from the falls. It seemed that, when the fire broke out, two gunners and a galley-boy attempted to launch the boat and it had capsized. Assistant Steward Morton, serving one of the guns, had also disappeared.

It was thought that he had been washed overboard by the cascades of water from near misses.

It was very quiet now. Most of the crew were asleep. Only the suspicion of a breeze rustled the surface of the dark Mediterranean.

At 2 a.m., a star of brilliant light blazed in the darkness ahead.

Lieutenant Barton gripped the captain's arm. 'The convoy's catching it again,' he said.

More parachute flares lit up and hung brilliantly in the sky. Then the crash of heavy firing began.

'I expect it's E-boats,' said Barton. 'Let's hope it isn't the whole Eytie fleet. It strikes me we're better off out here after all.'

III

Just before midnight the head of the convoy had reached Cape Bon and turned south on a course close to the Tunisian coast.

The British ships were now in the narrowest part of the channel with a hostile shore on one side and a minefield on the other.

The three TSD destroyers led the van, streaming paravanes to sweep any mines which might have been laid in the channel.

This precaution was soon fully justified for *Ashanti*, *Kenya* and *Manchester*, who were following with the only two merchant ships remaining in visual touch, *Melbourne Star* and *Wairangi*, all sighted loose mines bobbing in the sea close to them.

Two passed down the side of the *Ashanti*, so near that the lookouts were able to see their horns, which if touched would detonate them.

It was very quiet now, the darkest hour of the night.

—

The only sounds to be heard were the dull beat of engines and the rustle of water at the bows. The lookouts strained their eyes trying to pierce the darkness ahead.

On *Ashanti*'s bridge the telephone buzzer sounded:

'Radar plots bearing Red 5. Looks like small boats,' said a voice.

'Fire with everything you've got, on the radar plot,' the captain ordered.

Simultaneously, the whirr of a starter and the roar of a high-speed engine could be heard out to port. A starshell fired by *Kenya* burst high in the air, flooding the sea with a dim light.

'E-boats to port,' came half a dozen voices. The guns of all the British warships opened up together, tearing the calm sea into a lather around the dim forms of the E-boats.

These two MTBs, the first of four flotillas numbering nineteen boats which were waiting to receive the convoy between Cape Bon and Pantelleria, were both under way now. They dashed in to deliver their attacks, then, turning at high speed, began to lay smoke-screens to shield themselves from the withering fire. The British ships turned towards them to comb torpedo tracks.

The guns stopped firing, the E-boats were out of range. Five minutes later radar detected two more boats to starboard and the British engaged with a full broadside.

The enemy was temporarily driven off without loss to the convoy.

A running fight now developed with E-boats on both sides of the convoy. Fast motor-boats would come tearing in, fire their torpedoes, then retreat again behind smoke. Each time they were greeted with heavy fire and neither side scored any success.

At 1.20 a.m., when the battle was reaching its height and the regular gleam of the Kelibia light could be seen abeam, two E-boats, MS.16 and MS.22 of the Italian second flotilla, pressed home a courageous attack upon

Manchester, coming to within fifty yards of the cruiser before discharging their torpedoes.

Manchester went to full speed, turning hard to starboard and firing with both forward turrets, when there was a terrific explosion under the forward 4-inch gun deck as one of the torpedoes struck. With her steering locked the cruiser careered in a wide circle out of control, disappearing into the night.

Both engine-rooms were flooded and the after boiler-room damaged. All lights went out and the power was cut off. *Manchester* was now stopped and helpless and preparations were made for abandoning ship. The destroyer, *Pathfinder*, came alongside and took off 158 ratings and 5 injured men.

Meanwhile the E-boats had found the straggling remnant of the convoy which was following not far behind the warships.

Parted from the convoy, the master and lookouts on the bridge of the American *Santa Elisa* were peering into the darkness. Suddenly Captain Thompson saw the dark shape of an E-boat appear almost alongside the ship.

'See that son-of-a-bitch,' he shouted to Cadet Midshipman Francis Dales. 'Get him.'

Dales opened fire with the bridge Oerlikon. The sea creamed astern of the E-boat as she opened her throttle and then her guns began to spit back at the merchantman.

Dales's loader fell dead beside him but the cadet went on firing. The E-boat sprayed the bridge and smoke stack with bullets, and the captain and the naval liaison officer had to throw themselves to the deck to avoid being hit. Two more gunners were killed at their posts.

As Dales exhausted his ammunition, he saw that his adversary was on fire. In the same instant he spotted another E-boat dashing in from starboard. He reached for more ammunition, saw the E-boat fire a torpedo and then turn away in the darkness.

There was a terrific explosion as the torpedo struck

the starboard side of *Santa Elisa*'s No. 1 hold. Simultaneously, the petrol stacked everywhere went up with a roar and a blaze of flame. Dales saw men blown over the side by the force of it. Others were casting themselves into the sea.

As he ran with the captain to launch the boats, fire was engulfing the whole ship.

They managed to launch three of the boats and picked up as many survivors as they could find in the dark. Two hours later they were rescued by *Penn*.

Almeria Lykes had no chance to defend herself. She was following in the wake of two British destroyers when a torpedo fired by an unseen E-boat exploded on the port side of No. 1 hold and split the ship right across the deck in line with the forepeak bulkhead. The ship began to sink by the head and the engines failed. She was then abandoned.

A little later, the British ships *Wairangi* and *Glenorchy* were torpedoed. Both caught fire shortly after the crews had escaped. Most of these men and those from the *Almeria Lykes* were picked up by *Somali* and taken to Gibraltar.

It was now about 3.30 a.m., and at the head of the convoy the warships were fighting off another E-boat attack. As they were doing so they saw *Rochester Castle*, which had just regained contact with them, torpedoed out to starboard. Though heavily damaged forward, she succeeded in getting under way again shortly afterwards and soon worked up to a speed of thirteen knots.

Admiral Burrough had had no news of *Manchester* since she had been torpedoed. Accordingly, when *Charybdis* joined with *Somali* and *Eskimo* at 4.30 a.m., he dispatched the two destroyers to search for the cruiser.

The disastrous engagement with the E-boats had lasted until dawn. Altogether, eight Italian E-boats (Mas 552, 553, 554, 556, 557 and 564 and MS. 26 and 31) and two German (S.30 and S.36) had delivered fifteen attacks and although several had been damaged none were lost.

Now the admiral had only the cruisers, *Charybdis* and *Kenya* (which had a damaged bow), and a force of seven destroyers, to meet the Italian fleet.

As the sun rose, he fully expected to see the smoke of the enemy ships smudging the northern horizon and within a short time to feel the full weight of their salvoes to which, with his depleted force, he would have small chance of replying effectively.

The convoy would never reach Malta and the most he could do would be to inflict as much damage as possible before superior weight of metal pounded his cruisers and destroyers into blazing hulks.

CHAPTER ELEVEN

RAF Bluff the Italians

Dawn came slowly. First a tinge of eggshell-coloured light appeared in the east, changing to rose.

Aboard the flagship *Ashanti*, Admiral Burrough could see the barrels of the forward guns. Then the wires of the radio aerial were visible. Day was approaching.

The admiral was grey and drawn with sleeplessness. He knew that the testing time of his life was probably at hand. Soon he might have to order 2,000 men to action with the Italian fleet and most of them would die. He would almost certainly die with them.

Worse still, his mission would end in failure. After the warships had made their fruitless, suicidal attack, and after they had been beaten into blazing wrecks, the Italians would sail in and finish off the remaining merchantmen of the convoy at leisure. Malta would starve, another bastion of the British Empire would fall to the Axis and he knew what that might mean – at the best victory longer delayed, at the worst defeat.

Other officers on the bridge were already scanning the northern horizon where the Italian fleet was due to appear. He would wait a little. It was too dark yet.

He paced slowly down to the wing of the bridge. The flecks in the sea were becoming visible. He turned and raised his glasses unhurriedly to the north.

For a full ten minutes, he scanned the skyline. There were no smudges of hostile smoke, no long grey shapes or even the blobs of warships' top-hamper showing above the arc of the sea in the growing light. His hopes rose buoyantly in the gust of relief. Somehow the Italians had failed to rendezvous with their kill.

A combination of many factors had saved the convoy

and its escort from destruction at this stage of the operation. Chief among them was a psychological attitude which was to dog the Italian Navy throughout the war. From the start of hostilities, a general order of the Italian High Command sapped the will to attack and placed even the most determined admiral in an intolerable position.

This order, issued in September 1940, completely renounced the initiative. It read:

'Naval actions occur for one of two reasons: first, an encounter between two enemy squadrons, one of which seeks to prevent the other from fulfilling its mission; second, determined search by one squadron for the enemy fleet with the purpose of destroying it. The first situation may develop unexpectedly: in such a case the Italian Navy, if it has a chance of success, will fight with extreme resolution. The second alternative is not open to us because we are the weaker. To conceive of a battle as an end in itself is an absurdity not worth discussing.'

Since the destruction of the enemy might be considered the only way of gaining complete control of the sea, the Italian Supermarina's overall naval plan, if it had one, was faulty from its basis.

Added to this, the destruction of Italian ships at Taranto by the British fleet torpedo aircraft had made the Italian naval command highly nervous of putting to sea with heavy elements unless they received strong air protection. As the Italian fleet steamed at speed towards the convoy which they might confidently have expected to destroy, a top-ranking conference was taking place between the Axis commanders in Rome. The Italian naval staff, with the British attack on Taranto still in mind and also intelligence that a torpedo strike against their fleet was being planned at Malta, demanded air cover for their ships. They specified that they could not steam south of Pantelleria into waters covered by aircraft from Malta unless they were given this protection.

Such fighter cover would have to be provided by the Germans as the Italians had insufficient suitable long-range fighters. Field-Marshal Kesselring, as Commander-in-Chief Air South, was therefore asked to make sufficient German fighters available.

All ranks of the German Air Force were already filled with indignation against the Italian Navy over their conduct during the previous mid-June convoy. They held that their own good work on this occasion had been denied a fully successful outcome by what they considered to be a pusillanimous withdrawal by the Italian fleet when the complete destruction of convoy and escort had been within their power.

Moreover, Kesselring and his subordinates had, in the opinion of their own Admiral Weichold, 'a bigoted view of air results which had a bad effect on operational decisions'.

The German air commander refused point blank to grant the Italians' request, giving as his reason the need to protect his own bombers during the operation. An acrimonious argument ensued, with both sides firmly digging in their toes. Despite efforts by the Italian Commander-in-Chief, Cavallero, to compose their differences, the row reached a deadlock at which it was evident that the fighters would have to be used either for the fleet or the bombers, and could not be divided between the two.

Vital minutes ticked by, but the deadlock remained. Finally, in desperation, Cavallero proposed that Mussolini be asked to give a casting vote. After much more argument this course was adopted and the Italian Commander-in-Chief telephoned the Duce.

This enforced role of umpire in an explosive situation placed Mussolini in a quandary. He did not like to come out in blatant opposition to Kesselring for fear of offending Hitler or of appearing to favour Italian interests unduly; yet politically he would have welcomed a successful action by the Italian fleet. Finally, he gave in to the Germans and air cover was denied the Italian ships.

The two Italian cruiser divisions pressed on, however, towards their dawn interception with the convoy. Meanwhile, the RAF at Malta had taken a hand.

Air reconnaissance had detected enemy fleet movement as early as the evening of the 11th of August when the Italian Seventh Cruiser Division, comprising *Eugenio*, *Montecuccoli* and *Attendolo*, escorted by eleven destroyers, were sighted leaving Cagliari Harbour in Sardinia by Beaufighters returning from airfield raids. The following morning RAF pilots had seen the Fifth Division, *Gorizia* and *Bolzano* leave Messina. Later they were observed joining forces with *Trieste* which had come from the north.

When a Baltimore aircraft reported the rendezvous of the two divisions fifty miles north-west of Ustica at 7 p.m. it was plain that an attack on the convoy was planned and that it was likely to begin at dawn.

The RAF were in some difficulty. Air Vice-Marshal Sir Keith Park had been promised the use of a force of Middle East Liberators. These were not available and he had insufficient aircraft to mount an effective strike against the Italian fleet.

He therefore decided upon a stratagem. In the absence of proper means of attack perhaps the enemy could be frightened into turning back.

Wellington 'O for Orange' was dispatched at last light to take up the search and located the cruisers still steaming south. The pilot was then ordered to drop flares over the fleet. Wellington 'Z for Zebra' was also ordered to illuminate and attack with bombs. When this had been carried out 'Zebra's' pilot was told to send a signal in plain language directing imaginary aircraft to the scene.

This seemed to be partially successful, for the signal was picked up by the enemy and by 2.30 a.m. the cruisers had altered course towards the north-east.

To speed the parting guest, Park then sent another plain language message: 'Report result of your attack and latest enemy position for Liberators — most immediate.'

Then again, at 3.45 a.m., Wellington 'Y for Yorker' was ordered in plain language: 'Contact cruisers — illuminate and attack.'

All these plain language messages were picked up by the Italians, as was intended, and probably reinforced the decision by Supermarina to recall the cruisers. At the same time, fortune, in the guise of the Italo-German row over air cover, was the principal reason for abandoning what must have been a decisive attack. Almost within striking distance of the convoy, they turned back.

The story of this ill-judged fleet manœuvre did not end there. The British had another rude shock in store for the Italians.

When 'Pedestal' passed through the Straits of Gibraltar, the submarine, Unbroken, captained by Lieutenant Alastair Mars, was ordered to patrol two miles north of Cape Milazzo lighthouse which lay eighteen miles west of Messina naval base. After being repeatedly hunted and depth-charged by the enemy in this uncomfortable spot, Lieutenant Mars decided to vary the instructions he had been given. After a careful appraisal of the situation he came to the conclusion that a position half-way between the islands of Panaria and Salina was the best point at which to intercept any cruisers using the port of Messina. He turned a 'blind eye' to the fact that if he had miscalculated he was in for trouble, for the new position was thirty miles away from his ordered patrol line.

Early on the 12th he received a signal from Vice-Admiral, Malta: 'Enemy cruisers coming your way.'

Since 'your way' meant his proper position thirty miles away to the south, Mars was now faced with a difficult decision. Should he steam south to his official patrol line which he could not reach before the cruisers passed it, or should he remain where his own judgement told him the course of the cruisers was likely to lie?

Trying not to think about courts-martial, he stayed where he was.

At breakfast time, hydrophone echoes of heavy ships were heard approaching from the west.

Mars swung the periscope, and in the dawn light saw three or four cruisers in line ahead coming straight for him. He manœuvred for attack. He dived under the destroyer screen, missing one of the vessels by a hair's breadth, and then, with an 8-inch cruiser as target, fired three torpedoes.

As they spiralled down into deep waters to avoid the counter-attack, the men of *Unbroken* heard two loud explosions.

The heavy cruiser, *Bolzano*, was seriously damaged and played no further part in the war. The light cruiser, *Attendolo*, had her bows blown off and was many months repairing at Messina.

Two hundred miles to the south-westward, the sun shone over the convoy.

Five merchant ships, *Melbourne Star*, *Waimarama*, *Rochester Castle*, *Port Chalmers* and *Dorset*, had now been rounded up. *Brisbane Star* had reported that she was still making thirteen knots astern of them.

Then, as the sun rose higher and friendly Beaufighters and long-range Spitfires from Malta flew in to protect them, *Ledbury*, followed by *Ohio*, hove in sight.

'I knew we could rely on *Ledbury*,' Admiral Burrough signalled.

Then the battered tanker, 'sailing like a yacht' despite the great rent in her port side, took station once again astern of the line of convoy.

The admiral's worries were by no means over. To begin with, he doubted whether the air cover which had been promised to his force from Malta during that day could be used efficiently. The only two very high frequency radio sets which had been supplied to the convoy for directing the fighter cover were aboard *Nigeria* and

Cairo, the one damaged and out of action, the other sunk.

The lack of any air force intervention during the previous dusk air attack was evidently due to the fact that both these sets were immobilized when the two cruisers were struck by the enemy.

In fact, six Beaufighters of 248 Squadron had arrived on patrol over the convoy at about the time the cruisers were torpedoed. Receiving no further directions, this flight repeatedly dived from 5,000 feet in an attempt to find out what was going on. On each occasion they were fired on by their own ships.

Finally, they had returned to base without being able to assist the convoy in any way.

To prevent this happening again, Admiral Burrough's flag lieutenant worked through the night trying to improvise a suitable set.

With the help of the signals officer, Flags had finished his home-made set by the time the first Beaufighters appeared on the scene shortly after dawn and an air plotting board had been set up. Malta had been asked to arrange for the Beaufighters to work on a high frequency of 5,570 kilocycles which was the best they had been able to improvise.

For more than an hour he stood on the bridge of *Ashanti* shouting the call sign 'Bacon-Apples' into the microphone or listening intently for some answering call. Sometimes his face would light up with expectation, only to be quickly followed by a look of disappointment. Suddenly his face wreathed in smiles and he began a conversation in code which was quite unintelligible to the admiral or anyone else on the bridge. At frequent intervals he glanced at the Beaufighters in the sky, then down again at the plot, for he was trying to give the aircraft a course to steer to intercept the enemy snoopers which had already appeared. Unfortunately the Beaufighters did not seem to understand. They went cruising on without any apparent effort to obey his instructions. After more guarded conversation in code, the flag lieutenant's face wrinkled in despair and he flung down the microphone with an oath. He had just discovered that he was not talking to a Beaufighter at all but to the cruiser *Charybdis*.

After this noble effort, wireless contact had to be abandoned, and so it was that when the full force of the enemy's Sicilian air fleet fell upon Force X, they were without any means of fighter direction.

CHAPTER TWELVE

A 'Sitting Duck'

Ohio's gunners squinted into the rising sun, waiting for the attack which they knew might materialize at any moment.

Enemy spotting planes had followed them since first light until a flight of Beaufighters arrived from Malta to chase them away.

To the north-west and now slipping behind them, the two rounded hills on the Island of Pantelleria, fifteen miles away, could be clearly seen. Malta was still over 170 miles distant and, owing to the hard-fought night battles, the convoy was not yet within effective range of the majority of the fighters from the island.

As Mason received a signal to prepare for action against an incoming raid the drone of the approaching planes could be heard. Then he saw three Italian Savoia aircraft flying low down the side of the convoy, well out of range.

A shout from Pumpman Collins, at lookout on the poop, brought Bofors and Oerlikon barrels swinging quickly towards the stern as five Junkers 88s dived at the tanker. Accurate bursts of fire split the formation into jinking units and the bombs began to fall. Gray could see the whole black length of them as they left the aircraft and they gradually turned over, looking like footballs. Every second seemed an hour of time in a world of slow-motion. He flattened himself on the deck, but the bombs crashed into the sea harmlessly, well over to port.

Other aircraft were diving from the starboard beam, and Gunner Laburn calmly changed the barrel of the

Bofors gun as he turned towards the new attack, directing a withering and accurate fire on the new danger.
Once again the formation scattered, and *Ohio*, now the
chief target of the bombers had escaped unhurt.

This first attack of the day at 8 a.m. was being made
by twelve Junkers 88s, diving from 6,000 feet.

Two of them swept down on the *Waimarama* 200
yards in front of the *Ohio*. They came through the heavy
barrage which spotted the sky with black, white and
golden puffs. A stick straddled the merchant ship, scoring direct hits aft and forward. The 100 octane aviation
spirit stowed in the bridge deck took fire. She blew up
with a roar, disappearing in a sheet of flame and clouds
of billowing smoke, rising higher and higher with more
violent explosions as the cargo of shells and other
combustibles ignited. The second attacking enemy
plane disintegrated in the heart of the flame.

Melbourne Star was following close astern of *Waimarama*. Her master, Captain MacFarlane, and other members of the crew took cover as the ship was showered
with huge pieces of debris. A steel plate, five feet long,
fell on board. The base of a ventilator, half an inch thick
and two and a half feet high partly demolished one of
the machine-gun posts, and a piece of angle-iron at the
same moment narrowly missed one of their cadets. A 6-
inch shell fell on the roof of the captain's day cabin.

Ahead of the *Melbourne Star*, which carried the same
dangerous cargo as the stricken ship, the sea was a mass
of fire, spreading every moment wider and wider to
engulf them. Captain MacFarlane put the helm hard
aport, but the approaching furnace of heat drove him
from the monkey island down to the bridge. Blinded by
smoke and flame he shouted to the men to go forward
for he expected the ship to blow up at any moment.

Flames all round them now were leaping mast high
and the heat was terrific. The air became dryer and
harder to breath every minute as the oxygen was burned
out of it. The paint on the ship's sides took fire, and the

bottoms of the lifeboats were reduced to charcoal. For what seemed hours, but could only have been a matter of seconds, the ship ploughed through the holocaust, then she was clear and the blaze receded astern.

As the men resumed their stations it was found that thirty-six men were missing. Thinking that the forward end of the ship had been struck, and expecting her to blow up, they had jumped over the side.

Ohio, with a damaged steering gear and gaping kerosene tanks was also making straight for the flames. Mason was shouting: 'Hard a-port! For God's sake, hard aport!' down the telephone to the first officer on the after-deck. Stephen, on the poop, saw the flames leap up ahead and thought they had been hit. He rushed to the ship's side and then shouted to Gray to port the helm.

At first the tanker did not answer. Flames loomed directly in her path, and the officers on the bridge waited tensely, measuring distances. At last she swung to port and just pulled clear.

The destroyer *Ledbury* now came racing from the screen. It seemed impossible that any man in the *Waimarama* could have lived through the explosion, and, indeed, 80 of the crew of 107 had perished; but as the destroyer approached the edge of the flaming petrol men could be seen struggling in the water and the shrieks of others inside the pool of flame could be heard. Despite the danger to his own ship, Lieutenant-Commander Roger Hill of *Ledbury* steamed on and ordered boats to be launched.

The courage of the men in the water was amazing. Though the rapidly spreading film of blazing petrol threatened to engulf them at any moment, they were singing and encouraging one another. As *Ledbury* passed some of them, the captain spoke to them through the loudhailer explaining that he must get those nearest the flames first.

'That's all right, sir,' and 'Yes, get them first,' they shouted back, and went on singing. It was impossible to lay the ship's whaler, in charge of Gunner Musham, close enough to the flames: but men could be seen beyond in islands of unfired sea. Roger Hill immediately decided to take the destroyer in, and ordered rescue nets to be rigged along the ship's sides.

Slowly *Ledbury* edged in to the blaze, and to Admiral Burrough away in the convoy it seemed that she plunged straight in. The ship was given up for lost.

Petty Officer Cook went over the side again and again on a line to pick up men in the water.

Ledbury went astern and edged out again. Four times she plunged into the blazing sea in an attempt to get at men who still seemed to be alive.

One man could be seen, badly burnt, on a raft well within the circle of flame. *Ledbury* went in yet again, and this time she was enveloped from stem to stern in fire. She swung the wrong way and missed the raft. She circled round and re-entered the flames. Officers-Servant Reginald Sida volunteered to go over the fo'c'sle and take a line to the man on the burning raft. As he dived overboard he knew that the ship might have had to retreat leaving him at any moment. He reached the raft, carefully placed a life-saving belt round the injured man and then both were pulled to safety.

No other survivors being visible in the flames, *Ledbury* backed out again and began picking up survivors beyond the petrol patches.

The destroyer had passed one of them a number of times. On each occasion he bobbed up in the water and knuckled his forehead shouting 'Don't forget the diver, sir!' He was picked up, and turned out to be Bosun J. Cook who had jumped overboard from *Melbourne Star*.

The senior surviving officer of *Waimarama*, Radio Officer Jackson, had an extraordinary tale to tell. He was crossing to the starboard side of the bridge to bear a hand with the guns when the bombs struck, two aft, one abaft the bridge and one forward.

A great wall of flame leapt up in front of him. He

turned, but could not see the gun mounting he had just left no more than two yards away. There were flames all round him.

Instinctively he ducked into the bridge deck-house and ran down the ladder gaining the boat deck through a hole where the door had been. He clambered over a pile of debris with difficulty as the ship was listing sharply to starboard and saw about twenty men struggling in the water. The ship was sinking rapidly, and, apart from the corner on which he stood, completely enveloped in flames. The sea, too, was blazing all around except for the patch where the men were swimming. Shielding his eyes from the fire, he ran to the side and jumped overboard.

He could not swim, he was swallowing water and everything began to go black. In a sort of haze, he saw that the ship had swung round and the bows appeared to be falling down on top of him.

Somehow, he managed to struggle away, and when he looked round the ship had disappeared.

He lay on his back for a few minutes trying to decide what to do. The flames and black smoke were closing in on him. At that moment he saw Cadet Treves swimming towards him. The cadet, without any attempt to save himself from the oncoming wall of fire, helped Jackson to keep afloat until they came to a piece of wood which the non-swimmer could cling to.

Jackson, holding tight to the piece of wood, began to propel himself away from the burning petrol by kicking his feet, but to his horror the flames began to catch up with him. The heat was terrific and he decided that when the fire reached him he would undo his life-jacket and slip under. It was not to be. A fluke in the wind turned the blazing petrol aside and for two hours he floated until picked up by *Ledbury*.

Cadet Treves, whose action had saved Jackson's life, was also picked up.

Away to the south-east, the convoy steamed on

towards Malta, and under his care Admiral Burrough could number now only the merchant ships *Ohio*, *Port Chalmers*, *Melbourne Star*, *Dorset* and *Rochester Castle*, formed up in two columns.

Although the roundelled wings of Malta Spitfires and Beaufighters could be seen high above in the brassy sky, the admiral knew that the enemy had not yet developed the full power of his air attack from the nearby Sicilian airfields. The severest test was at hand.

On the bridge of *Ohio*, Captain Mason and Lieutenant Barton scanned the skies until their eyes ached. They knew that it was 'any time now'.

The R/T crackled: 'Stand by for dive-bombing attack.' Ahead, tiny dots in the sky could be seen, circling. The alarm bells rang and the gun crews swung their guns restlessly, waiting for the strike.

It came at 9.25 a.m., the most determined attack they had yet encountered, from more than sixty black Stuka dive-bombers escorted by Italian fighters, and *Ohio* was the main target.

One after another the dive-bombers peeled off and came down. As the menacing 'W' shapes of the wings got bigger and bigger, the howl of the engines and panic-provoking sirens reached a crescendo. The bombs thundered down, spraying *Ohio* with great gouts of water tossed from the sea, and the aircraft raced by at mast height, machine-guns chattering as they jinked this way and that to avoid the heavy counter-fire.

They seemed to come from every quarter, and Mason and Barton on the bridge now ducked instinctively only at the last minute when the danger seemed most acute.

One exceptionally near miss sent an avalanche of water over the foredeck. The ship shuddered violently. A few minutes later the captain received a report that the plates had buckled and that the forward oil tank had filled with water.

—

The 6-inch gun at the bows twisted in its mounting and was put out of action.

At the after-end of the ship, Pumpman Collins, who was serving the guns endlessly with his home-made ammunition hoist, saw his friend Ginger Leach walking calmly aft, scorning to duck as successive waves of Stukas flashed by.

'Bleeding murder, ain't it?' Ginger said laconically.

Every gun of the *Ohio* blazed away continually. Barrels grew red hot and had to be changed, but the protective barrage slackened.

On the bridge, the Bofors gun had been in action for nearly half an hour. Gunner Billings, peering over the sights with red-rimmed eyes, saw a Junkers 87 snaking into the attack, lower and coming closer than his companions had dared. He pressed the trigger again. The shells were hitting the black fuselage, bits were dropping off. 'Got her,' Billings shouted, still pressing the trigger.

The plane crashed straight into *Ohio*'s starboard side forward of the upper bridge and exploded. Half a wing slammed into the upper-work of the bridge and a rain of aircraft parts showered her from stem to stern. The bomb, which Billings had unconcernedly watched as it left the aircraft, fortunately failed to explode.

The men on the bridge got off their knees, looked at one another and laughed as if it had been a big joke.

Steward Meeks, quite unperturbed, appeared at the top of the bridge ladder with a kettle of coffee and sandwiches.

'Hot work, sir,' he commented, handing the captain a pint mug. Mason suddenly realized that this was the second time the chief steward had appeared with food and drink since the action had begun.

On the poop, Stephen was diving under the same water tank every time an attack developed. Each time he thought: 'If that tank shifts, I'll be crushed,' but he continued to take shelter under it. The attack was dulling the men's minds. They were getting 'bomb happy'. They laughed inanely when near-missed, but the guns kept on firing and firing accurately, the ammunition continued to come up from the magazines, *Ohio* steamed on towards Malta.

Their luck couldn't last. The guns turned to meet twenty Junkers 88s diving in from ahead, dropping parachute mines, torpedoes and circling torpedoes. The ship turned slowly to comb torpedoes. Then came the bombs. Two sticks of them burst down either side of *Ohio*. The ship lifted and went on lifting, until her bottom was out of the water. Cascades of spray and bomb splinters lashed the deck. Then she fell back with a teeth-shaking crash.

Down in the engine-room, it seemed to the chief, Jimmy Wyld, as if the ship had suddenly become airborne. This was a totally new experience. Automatically his hand went to shut off steam, but the special differential gearing had slowed the propeller automatically. It occurred to him that in another ship a screw racing so far out of the water would have shaken the engines out of her.

Mechanically he checked over the engine-room. Nothing was damaged, but it couldn't last. Every few minutes the nearby concussion of bombs clanged on the ship's sides like giant hammers. Sooner or later one would find its mark, but somehow this self-evident conclusion did not seem to worry him at all.

A gigantic crash to starboard sent *Ohio* reeling to port. The engine-room lights went out and they were in darkness. There were simultaneous shouts for torches, but before the groping engineers could find them, Electrician Higgins had felt his way to the master switches which had been thrown out by the violence of the explosion and turned the lights on again.

This time the ship had not escaped damage. The boiler fires had blown out and it was a race against time to restore them before the steam dropped too low to work the fuel pumps.

With practised co-operation the engineers went to work. Fuel starter torches were lighted to refire the furnaces. The complicated routine of restarting the engine went forward smoothly, and within twenty minutes *Ohio* was steaming at sixteen knots.

Then another salvo of bombs shook every plate in the ship. Once more the engine-room lights went out and the engines slowed, shivered and stopped.

When Higgins succeeded in switching on emergency lighting he found that the main switch had been torn off the bulkhead. More seriously still, the electric fuel pumps had been broken by the concussion.

The bridge telephone rang and Captain Mason's voice asked: 'Anything serious, Chief?'

'Looks bad, sir,' Wyld replied. 'Pumps have gone. We'll get her going again somehow.'

'Good luck,' Mason answered. 'We'll try to keep 'em off up here.'

The engineers went to work trying to forget the hollow crashes of bombs falling close by and the stark fact that at any moment the sea might invade the dimly lit trap of the engine-room.

The floor plates were removed, and Wyld and Buddle, the second engineer, crawled through the bilges to the valves which would connect up the steam fuel pumps to replace the broken electrical system.

Meanwhile the junior engineer, Harry Sless, the only Jew anyone could remember in a ship's engine-room, took on one of the most dangerous jobs, wriggling his way over the boiler casing looking for fractures and checking for oil in the water.

The steam auxiliary system was connected to the pumping mechanism. Wyld and Buddle emerged from the bilges covered with oil and slime. The critical moment had arrived. Was there still steam to pump oil into the fires? Wyld watched the gauges and gave the order. Grinstead, the third engineer, thrust the flaming starter torch into the cooling darkness of No. 1 furnace.

With a hollow 'woof' the vaporised oil under low pressure exploded, blowing out the sides of No. 1 boiler and filling the engine-room with black smoke.

In the murky half light, they tried again. This time the other boiler fired properly, and life began to come back to the engines. Wyld, watching the revolution counter, saw the indicator climb slowly to five, ten, fifteen and then waver at twenty. The bridge telephone shrilled.

'She's making alternate black and white smoke,' came Mason's voice. 'No more than four knots at the moment.'

'Ay, oil in the water somewhere,' Wyld replied.

'We're losing vacuum in the condenser,' Buddle shouted.

Wyld relayed the information to the captain.

At that moment the engines stopped.

'It's all over, lad, I'm afraid. In five minutes we won't have steam to steer her. Sorry.' Wyld turned away from the controls and went to close the engine sea cocks.

Ohio lost way slowly and came to a stop, rolling slightly in the small beam swell. A pair of Stukas screamed down, wavered in the face of the determined fire and dropped their bombs short. The ship was now a 'sitting duck', and an easy target.

Malta, with her life in the balance, and *Ohio* with her vital cargo, seemed very far apart.

CHAPTER THIRTEEN

Ohio Abandoned

Parrying every form of air attack, Admiral Burrough in *Ashanti* led the convoy on towards Malta. *Ohio* was immobilized far astern and SS *Dorset*, straddled by a stick of bombs, lay similarly crippled while her engineers struggled manfully in the forlorn hope of repairing extensive blast damage and pumping out the flooded engine-room.

The admiral's protective screen of warships had been further reduced. *Ledbury* was picking up *Waimarama* survivors in the blazing sea, and destroyers *Penn* and *Bramham* had been sent to assist *Ohio* and *Dorset*. The destroyers *Eskimo* and *Somali* were miles away looking for *Manchester* survivors.

So, to protect the remaining merchantmen, *Port Chalmers*, *Melbourne Star* and *Rochester Castle*, strung out in line astern, he now had only *Ashanti*, the cruisers *Kenya* and *Charybdis*, and the destroyers *Intrepid*, *Icarus*, *Fury* and *Pathfinder*.

The earlier Stuka attacks had been partly frustrated by the fierce 'Umbrella' barrage, but, lacking an outer screen, Admiral Burrough grimly calculated that if the enemy attacked with torpedo bombers there would be small means of keeping them at a safe distance.

The first torpedo strike came at 10.50 a.m., when twelve Italian bombers were sighted flying in low on the port beam. The cruisers immediately engaged them with their heavy armament, but the enemy airmen pressed home their attack. At the same moment another higher flying group of aircraft released parachute mines and circling torpedoes.

Sirens boomed and the ships heeled into a sharp

emergency turn. The mines and circling torpedoes fell
all round the ships, but none were hit. The torpedo
attack was partly foiled by the quick turn and heavy
barrage, but *Port Chalmers* had an almost miraculous
escape. One torpedo passed right under her. Then her
master, Captain H. G. B. Pinkney, noticed heavy vi-
bration on the wire of the starboard paravane. Paravanes
are submerged floats towed from the bows of a ship by
wires which stream out at an angle and protect the
ship's sides from mines; when *Port Chalmers*'s crew
had almost wound in their paravane wire, they found
that the float had caught an unexploded torpedo.

With this lethal 'fish' firmly hooked to the ship, the
master sent a frantic signal to *Ashanti*: 'What shall we
do with this?'

His predicament was a dangerous one. To let go the
paravane might immediately explode the torpedo close
to the ship's side. Similarly, the torpedo might also
explode if he went ahead to veer the paravane away from
the ship.

Admiral Burrough, who could now plainly see the
fouled torpedo, ordered him to stop the ship, let her
slowly gather sternway, and then cut the paravane adrift
when it was as far away as the wire would take it.

Slowly *Port Chalmers* went astern until the paravane
and its deadly companion lay about a hundred yards
ahead. As the wire was cut there was a gigantic explosion, but a swift examination showed that there had
been no damage and the convoy sailed on.

As another dive-bombing attack was being beaten off,
a column of water shot up close to *Kenya*'s bows. The
cruiser slowed to ten knots and signalled the flagship
that her forward engine-room was on fire. After 20
minutes of anxiety, however, the fire was put out and
Kenya was steaming with the convoy again at 16 knots.

Despite considerable difficulties, the Malta-based
long-range Spitfires and Beaufighters were giving fleet

and convoy some protection, but the Axis formations were coming out from Sicily at low level and could not easily be picked up by radar. The intercepting planes, without communication with the ships, were frequently unable to engage their opponents before the attacks developed. Four enemy planes, however, were shot down and seen to fall into the sea. Admiral Burrough also noticed that a number of formations broke up and turned for home without making an attack.

The close-range Spitfires, now reinforced by the 36 flown in from the carrier *Furious* in 'Operation Bellows', were still unable to reach the convoy, but they carried out sweeps towards Sicily and succeeded in intercepting some of the attacking aircraft.

In addition, a Wellington bomber circled the stricken *Ohio* in case the Italians should hazard a daylight E-boat attack.

Another friend of *Ohio* was also about to come to her aid. *Ledbury* had finished picking up survivors from *Waimarama* and had increased to full speed to join the convoy thirty miles ahead. She sent a signal to Admiral Burrough:

INTERROGATIVE STOP REJOIN OR GO HOME

When the signal rating handed Commander Roger Hill the admiral's reply, he found that the code groups of the message had been received corruptly. He was apparently ordered to proceed to the Orkney and Shetland Islands! The captain and his number one, Lieutenant Anthony Hollins, considered the signal. It was plainly intended as an order to return to Gibraltar, but they might be forgiven for not interpreting it correctly. Ahead of them lay *Ohio*, the ship they had led back to the convoy the previous night, and consequently both men had a proprietary feeling about her. Now she was alone, evidently in trouble, and exposed to the full force of the air attack. Plainly it was *Ledbury*'s duty to go to the assistance of the tanker. So, as a great seaman had done before him,

Roger Hill turned a blind eye to the signal and set course for *Ohio*.

As she approached the tanker was making less than two knots and great gouts of alternate black and white smoke were pouring from her funnel.

The destroyer ranged alongside and Hill shouted an offer of a tow to Captain Mason. At that moment, the engines finally expired with a great puff of black smoke.

Ohio presented a sad sight. She was low in the water, there was a great rent in her port side and daylight could be seen streaming in from the starboard. Paint was scorched and blackened where the fire had taken a hold and her deck upper-works and smoke stack were so peppered with machine-gun bullets and splinters that they looked like colanders.

The fuselage of the broken German bomber lay on the forepeak and one of the wings straddled the side of the bridge. Aircraft parts, shell and bomb splinters were strewn on her decks, so that it was difficult to walk without stepping on them.

The men were bleary and red-eyed and almost asleep at their posts, but when a Junkers 88 came out of the sun towards them, the gun-barrels swung swiftly on to the target and the stiff defensive fire caused the pilot to drop his stick of bombs short of the destroyer and tanker. Battered, battle-scarred and disabled she might be and the men dazed and tired, but *Ohio* could still hit back.

At this critical moment in Malta's destiny, *Ledbury* stood by the crippled tanker as successive waves of enemy bombers dived in to finish off so valuable a prize. The addition of her guns probably tipped the scales between victory and defeat, for in each case the enemy was beaten off. Then the destroyer *Penn* arrived with orders to take over the protection of *Ohio* and, if possible, tow her to Malta. The alternative was to take off her crew and scuttle her, for at all costs so valuable a cargo had to be denied to the enemy.

As the captains of the two destroyers were concerting

arrangements for the tow, *Ledbury* intercepted a signal from Vice-Admiral Leatham in Malta, suggesting that she should be sent to look for the missing cruiser *Manchester*, for at this stage he did not know that she had sunk.

Regretfully, Roger Hill set course for Cape Bon. He did not know it then but he was soon to see *Ohio* again.

As *Ledbury* sped away westwards towards the African coast, where *Manchester* had last been seen, Lieutenant Commander J. H. Swain, RN, edged *Penn* alongside the battered *Ohio*.

'I'm going to try to tow you out of this, Captain,' shouted Commander Swain. 'Can you take a 10-inch manilla?'

Captain Mason waved assent and dispatched a party forward under the second officer, McKilligan. It took them nearly twenty minutes to clear away part of the cockpit of the crashed German aircraft and the other debris from the bitts to which they meant to attach the towing line.

When all was ready Mason signalled the destroyer. *Penn* ranged slowly alongside, then a rating on the stern flung a heaving line. Quickly they began to haul in the tow. The heavy manilla rope came over the side, and as it did so a German bomber came howling out of the sun. The men flung themselves to the deck as two near-misses deluged the fo'c'sle with water. The brisk return fire, however, drove off the raider, and the men began once more to heave in the rope.

At last the tow was secured with four turns round the bitts, and the captain signalled *Penn* that all was now ready. Slowly, the destroyer began to go ahead. The rope tightened, shedding a fine spray as the strands bit. With a jerk the destroyer stopped as the full weight of *Ohio* came upon her, then, ordering further revolutions she forged ahead again and *Ohio* began to move. The hull gathered way, and as it did so the great rent in her side began to turn her inexorably to port. Without motive power it was impossible to operate the steering gear to counteract this movement. *Penn* was straining on the tow at almost full revolutions. The bitts creaked and the rope stood straight and hard as an iron bar. Still *Ohio* turned until the destroyer was towing at an angle of ninety degrees.

The tanker came almost to a stop and her head began to pay off slowly in the direction of Malta. *Penn* tried again, but *Ohio* still turned away to port.

They were making no progress at all, in fact with the easterly wind they were drifting backwards.

Mason seized the loudhailer: 'It's no good,' he shouted. 'The only way is either to tow from alongside or with one ahead and another ship astern.'

'Where's the other ship coming from?' came back the reply. 'Let's have another try.'

On board *Ohio* the engineers, blackened, oil-stained and weary, came out on deck. They could do nothing now until a full inspection of the boilers could be made, and for that the casings would have to be allowed to cool. Even then, although they refused to entertain the idea, there was nothing that they could do, nothing, that is, without hours of time and spare parts, which lay many miles away.

All were in the last stages of exhaustion after their fight to keep *Ohio* moving, but all of them immediately volunteered to help serve the guns. Unfortunately, at this stage, many of the Oerlikons were temporarily out of action. The sudden cooling of barrels and mechanism by continual deluges of water from close bombs had caused all manner of minor stoppages and other damage. Many of them were already red with rust.

Grinstead, the third engineer, was almost all in. Down in the engine-room he had performed prodigies of strength and dexterity. Now he was to experience the full shock of air attack on deck. Wiping the grease from his face with an oily rag he asked Collins at the ammunition hoist: 'Where's the best place, Jumbo?'

'Where they ain't gonna drop,' said Collins. Then with sudden urgency: 'That's here. Quick. Get down.' The pumpman pulled Grinstead down beside him. As he did so a huge gout of water drenched them both. In eighteen inches of water, Grinstead was struggling to get up and retrieve his tin hat which had been washed off. Collins, wise from bitter experience, held on to him tightly. An 18 inch bomb splinter crashed down just in front of them – just where Grinstead would have been had he gone for the tin hat.

As the attack developed, *Penn* went to full speed to part the tow. At the end of the line she was a 'sitting duck' and, moreover, in a poor position to protect the tanker. The manilla snapped, frayed ends snaking back viciously, and the destroyer turned hard to port with all her guns blazing.

Another bomber came screaming down towards the *Ohio* from the starboard beam. The lower bridge Oerlikon opened up and the first few rounds were close. Then the gunner found the range and the aircraft disappeared with a crack into flying smoke and splinters. But in the split second before death had come to the German airmen the bomb-aimer had released his cargo. A bomb hit *Ohio* just under the water amidships, where the torpedo had already rent the side.

As water and splinters crashed down on the deck, Captain Mason could see the ship bend to port.

'I reckon that's broken her back,' he shouted grimly to Barton. Wearily he got up from the deck and made his way down to make an inspection.

The plates had opened farther. Now there was more water in the amidships section and it looked as though the adjoining tank was being flooded. The captain thought it was only a matter of time now. He straightened up and looked around him. The men were practically asleep. They had plainly reached that stage of exhaustion at which even the greatest danger could only

call forth a slow, sluggish movement. Many were
already nodding at their posts.

Gray, the first officer, still stood by the immobilized
steering engine, leaning his head, cushioned upon folded
arms, against the steel plates of the deck-house. He had
been on duty for more than thirty hours, first on the
bridge, then conning the ship from astern since she had
been torpedoed the day before.

The protecting destroyer, *Penn*, nosed her way almost
alongside, and the captain cupped his hands: 'There's
nothing we can do at the moment, I'm afraid,' he
shouted. 'We'll have to wait for dark. Why don't you
abandon ship for the present, and come aboard here?
You're just risking your lives to no good. You can go
back tonight.'

'I don't think she'll last that long,' Mason shouted
back. 'She's broken her back by the look of it. We'll
come aboard if you don't mind.'

He looked round the battered decks. So this was what
they had fought for all this time – to leave the ship, their
mission unaccomplished. He hated the idea, but the
destroyer captain was right. He gave the order to abandon ship.

With easy skill, *Penn* manœuvred alongside, until the
two ships were nearly touching. The crew of *Ohio*
mustered their last reserves of strength to jump on to
the destroyer's deck. When all had gone, Captain Mason
bade what he thought was likely to be a last farewell to
his ship, and followed them.

He looked mechanically at his watch as he did so. It
was still only 2 p.m.

Aboard *Penn* the decks were already crowded with
survivors from other merchant ships. The men of *Ohio*
sought out empty corners and dropped into immediate
slumber. Many of them could not be woken when the
stewards of the destroyer came round with tea.

The tanker now stood alone, deserted. She was low in

the water, and as *Penn* circled her slowly there was not one man who thought she would survive.

Meanwhile, *Ledbury* was racing westwards at speed in search of *Manchester*. So far, no word had been received from the destroyers *Eskimo* and *Somali* which had left five hours previously to look for her. These two ships had picked up part of the crew of the American merchantman *Almeria Lykes* and *Wairangi* before continuing with their search. Though abandoned, both of these merchantmen were still afloat, but the commanding officer of *Eskimo* did not sink them as he thought he might have an opportunity later of salvaging them. Close in to the Tunisian shore, *Eskimo* and *Somali* had found some of *Manchester*'s company on rafts and lifeboats, and they then learned for the first time that the cruiser had been scuttled upon the orders of her captain. Other survivors could be seen on the beach being marched away by French soldiers to internment. While these rescue operations were proceeding, an Italian plane circled and, instead of attacking the destroyers, dropped a raft near some swimmers. A German Junkers 88, which followed it, was not so gentlemanly. It machine-gunned both ships.

Having picked up all the men they could find, the two destroyers set course for Gibraltar, and it was then that they found among the survivors the four missing men from *Ohio*. According to them, they had launched a lifeboat as soon as the torpedo had struck, but in the process the lifeboat had capsized throwing them into the water. Later they had been picked up by *Manchester*, only to have to take to the boats once again.

All this was unknown to the captain of *Ledbury*, for he had received neither the signal reporting the sinking of the *Manchester* nor that detailing the picking up of her survivors. For some time, the signal staff in the destroyer had been showing signs of serious deterioration of efficiency in receiving and decoding messages. The reason was clear. They were desperately tired. As

with the crew of *Ohio*, and indeed, with the crew of
every ship in the fleet, the men in *Ledbury* were reaching the limit of their endurance. A number of them were
also suffering from painfully swollen ankles.

Commander Roger Hill realized that the fatigue of his
ship's company had reached a dangerous point. He
sought for a means of reviving them, and realized that
some surprise, some sudden success, that would wake
them up again was needed. A few minutes later the
opportunity occurred.

Two three-engined Italian torpedo-bombers came in
suddenly on the port beam. With only a split second to
weigh the consequences, Commander Hill rang the
cease-fire bells for the heavy 4-inch guns. He calculated
that if they held their fire the Italians might come close
enough for accurate shooting by the Oerlikons and light
armament before releasing their torpedoes. On came the
bombers. Their markings were plainly visible now. The
number one, Lieutenant Anthony Hollins, stared at the
captain as if he was mad. The captain ordered 'Hard
aport,' and, as he did so all the guns opened up together.
Flames burst from the port engines of one of the aircraft.
Then fire began to stream from the other. The crew
cheered as both plunged into the sea.

The captain's ruse had succeeded, but it nearly ended
in disaster. Torpedoes, launched by both aircraft, were
running towards them, and one almost scraped down
the side of the ship; but the crew were awake now.
Tiredness seemed to have fallen from them.

'I think we might splice the mainbrace. Don't you,
Number One?' said the captain with a grin. The signal
for splicing the mainbrace was solemnly hoisted, and
the coxswain and supply petty officer got up the rum.
This completed the cure for the time being.

As *Ledbury* pressed on, two columns of smoke
appeared on the horizon. They altered course towards
them, but as they approached they saw that it was

blazing oil and petrol marking the graves of two merchant ships sunk earlier that morning. Soon after they sighted the Tunisian coast through the thick heat haze. They had made an almost perfect landing, off the village of Hammamet.

They could not, of course, find any sign of *Manchester*. *Ledbury* cruised slowly down the coast, searching, and when she was off Ras-mahmur, the Vichy signal station at Neboel started calling up in Morse: 'VHM — VHA.' *Ledbury* made no reply. They had already hauled down their ensign as a precautionary measure. Farther down the coast at Hammamet the signal station there ran up a series of international flags, reading: 'Show your signal letters.' The captain immediately ordered the hoisting of an Italian group consisting of the flag 'I' and three other flags tied in knots so as to be unreadable. This seemed to satisfy the Frenchman, for he broke out a large French 'N' sign and there was no more communication.

Preparations were then made to bury the body of one of the men picked out of the burning sea during the morning. It had been sewn up in canvas, but there was difficulty about finding something to weight it down. The chief engineer refused point-blank to supply firebricks, which were usually used, for he was already short of them. Despite protests from the gunner's mate, an armour-piercing shell was used instead.

The body was buried with full military honours, a firing-party and a white ensign draped over the canvas-shrouded corpse, and Lieutenant Hollins read the funeral service.

For more than two hours *Ledbury* steamed up and down the coast searching, but could find nothing. Then they received a signal from RAF Reconnaissance that an Italian cruiser and two destroyers had been sighted off Zembra not much more than thirty miles to the northward of the destroyer. It was clearly time to go. The captain rang down for twenty-four knots and set course back to the eastward. He was determined to return to the assistance of *Ohio* if she still remained afloat.

Meanwhile, the leading ships of the convoy and their escort had experienced their last air attack. At 12.30 p.m. they came under the protection of the close range Spitfires from Malta. With more than a score of British planes patrolling, the Axis decided to call it a day.

Two hours later, the Malta force of mine-sweepers, commanded by Commander Jerome in *Speedy*, joined Admiral Burrough and took over responsibility for the convoy. *Rye* was detached to assist *Ohio*.

At 4 p.m. Admiral Burrough with Force X withdrew to the westward.

Preceded by mine-sweepers searching the channel, three battle-scarred ships, *Port Chalmers*, *Rochester Castle* and *Melbourne Star* whose sides were burned and blistered by the flames from *Waimarama* approached Valletta. They passed into the Grand Harbour at 6.18 p.m. to the cheers of the inhabitants lining the medieval ramparts.

Now, Malta had the food to sustain the siege, but, unknown to the jubilant Maltese, the position was as desperate as ever. Without *Ohio*'s cargo of oil and paraffin, the Island could not survive, and that cargo was still seventy miles away in an abandoned and apparently sinking ship.

CHAPTER FOURTEEN

Too Late to Save *Ohio*?

Rye to Vice-Admiral Malta:
JOINED PENN WITH MLS. 121 AND 168 STANDING BY
OHIO POSITION 36 DEGREES 00 MINUTES NORTH 12
DEGREES 59 MINUTES EAST 13/8 AT 1740 HOURS STOP
TOW WILL BE ATTEMPTED MESSAGE ENDS

On board HMS *Penn*, Chief Officer Stephen shook two
of the sleeping members of the tanker's crew: 'Captain
wants volunteers to go on board the ship again,' he said,
as they looked up sleepily.

Captain Mason, standing nearby, stiffened: 'Volunteers be damned,' he shouted. 'We've still got a crew,
haven't we?'

He sprang on to a water tank and cupped his hands.

'*Ohio, Ohio* – wakey wakey!'

Along the main deck of the destroyer the sleepers
were stirring now. They turned over and shook themselves, then slowly sat up like tired animals. As Mason
shouted again they looked towards him.

'Listen, men. The ship is still afloat. If you look out
there you'll see there's a mine-sweeper joined us. The
navy's going to tow us. It's our duty to be back there and
take that tow in. Shake it up now. We'll be alongside in
a minute, and I want everyone aboard.'

Slowly, the men got up, staggering a little with tiredness. Then they looked around them. Out on the starboard quarter lay *Ohio*, low in the water but still intact,
still floating. Circling slowly round her were the two
launches 121 and 168 and the fleet mine-sweeper *Rye*
from Malta. Aboard the mine-sweeper men were already
preparing the towing gear.

Penn came slowly alongside the battered tanker. Captain Mason was the first to jump aboard, and he was followed by the whole crew.

Without a word the engineers disappeared down the engine-room companionway. The gunners settled down behind their guns, cocked the mechanism and examined the magazines. The deck-hands were told off for various duties.

When they had abandoned the ship four hours before, they had been at the end of their tether. They could scarcely have fought the ship a moment longer. Now, after resting aboard the destroyer, a new spirit had surged up in them. Their bodies were tired but the will to resist had returned.

Chief Officer Gray had led a party forward and was prepared to receive the tow.

Down below, in the pitch dark, groping round the intricate mass of machinery with the aid of torches, the chief engineer, Jimmy Wyld, aided by Murray, the fourth, and Junior Engineer Sless, was checking valves and closing those which had been left open during the hurried abandonment of the ship.

At the after-end of the steering flat the second and third engineers, Buddle and Grinstead, were superintending the rigging of emergency steering gear, while Stephen, the third officer, stood by with four men at the one remaining telephone which connected with the bridge, waiting to operate it.

Meanwhile, Pumpman Collins and the storekeeper, 'Ginger' Leach, had been told off for a tough job.

In the darkness of the engine-room, feeling every foot of the way to make sure the gratings were still in position below their feet, they tried to locate two sets of chain blocks which had to be used on the relieving gear for the emergency steering. In this part of the engine-room behind the boilers there was a strong smell of ammonia, which happened to be Collins's pet aversion.

However, the search went on, both men holding their noses, and the blocks were finally located between two water tanks. Laboriously they dragged them to the steerage flat and, feeling rather pleased with themselves, for doing a job which would normally have occupied five or six men, they reported to the chief officer. Gray, however, was unimpressed:

'Where have you been? Stop to have a cup of tea?' he asked.

Out in the Mediterranean sunlight *Penn*'s tow had been made fast to *Ohio*. The destroyer went ahead, but once more the gaping hole in the tanker's side made her turn sharply to port. *Penn* slacked the tow. Then her captain hailed Mason: 'You'll have to get that rudder working,' he shouted over the loudhailer, 'we can't tow her like this.'

Mason phoned Stephen: 'For Christ's sake get that rudder cast off,' he shouted, 'or we'll never get to Malta.'

In the steering flat, engineers and deck-hands were struggling to rig the hand steering gear. The chains connecting the rudder to the now useless emergency steering engine were cast off. Cables were then attached to the chains and reeved through the relieving tackles. It was a heavy job yet somehow they managed to finish it in half an hour.

With the deck-hands manning the cables, Stephen phoned the bridge.

'All ready, sir. We've set the rudder to give her about five or six degrees to starboard. You can try now to tow.'

Captain Mason signalled *Penn*, and slowly the towing wire took the strain. The tanker began to forge forward again. The destroyer increased speed and now *Ohio* was going forward at five or six knots, with only a slight tendency to turn to port.

This speed, however, could not be maintained. A fluke of wind here or a fluke of tide there would begin to send the tanker into a turn and the destroyer at the end of her tow veering to starboard with her stern would be dragged inwards by the dead weight of the tanker.

Captain Mason phoned the steering flat: 'We're still swinging. Do you think you could steer her with the tackles?'

The reply was a sharp impolite negative. The tackles were too heavy.

Penn and *Rye* then had a short conference. A new plan was devised. *Rye* passed 300 fathoms of her sweep wire to the destroyer, who made it fast amidships. Both naval vessels went ahead again, *Rye* acting as a stabilizing factor for the destroyer. *Ohio* was soon towing again at between four and five knots, and the tendency to swing had been overcome.

Air activity had been unusually absent while these towing operations were going on, but shortly after 6.30 the ominous drone of engines could be heard and the gunners peered anxiously through the haze awaiting the inevitable attack. Mason ordered the engineers on deck as a safety precaution.

Unfortunately, the strike developed from astern. Four Junkers 88s came in at low level and the two towing naval vessels had difficulty in bringing their guns to bear. One bomb landed close astern of *Ohio*, immobilizing the rudder. As Mason ducked he saw that another would hit the ship.

It crashed through the fore-end of the boat deck, exploding on the boiler tops, forcing the engine-room staff out on deck. As they tumbled out of the engine-room companionway, coughing and choking, it could be seen that they were blinded with asbestos lagging off the top of the boiler. Their faces, clothes and hands were smothered with blue powder.

Simultaneously, an engine-room ventilator fell on to the Bofors gun.

The gun-crew picked themselves up and began burrowing frantically at the debris.

'There's a man under here,' someone shouted, and other members of the crew ran to help them.

Finally they dragged out the body of Gunner Brown, the gun trainer. He was still alive, but plainly critically injured internally.

Mason made another examination of the ship. The bomb had had a delayed action. It had pierced two decks and then blown most of the engine-room to pieces. Had he not just given orders to Wyld and his men to come on deck, many of them would have been killed. The rudder was now useless, and the tow had been cast off by the destroyer. Even a superficial examination of the rent amidships showed that the gap had widened and that *Ohio* had almost certainly broken her back. Two more air attacks were made and bombs fell close to both *Penn* and *Rye*. Cascades of water crashed aboard the fore-deck of *Ohio* as a stick narrowly missed her.

Once more Mason gave the order to abandon ship and the two motor launches, anticipating this, were already alongside.

Despite a continuous air attack the crew left the ship in an orderly fashion. First the injured gunner was lowered slowly over the side on a stretcher, then, one by one, the crew left.

The chief engineer went to his own quarters and grabbed a bag. On deck he found the captain with the ship's papers. 'I suppose this is the finish?' said Wyld.

'I'm afraid so. Anyhow, we'll have to get off her for the present.'

Wyld went over the side, and Mason had a last look round to make sure that no one was left behind. As he reached the rail again, he hesitated.

'Hurry up,' said the commander of the motor launch. 'I want to get away from here. It doesn't look too healthy.'

'I think I'm going to stop,' Mason replied.

'Don't be a bloody fool. You can't do any good there.

She'll be sinking any moment,' said the ML captain.
Mason knew he was right. There was little chance that
Ohio would outlast the night. He threw his case over
the side into the launch and quickly followed it.

Night, bringing the blessed relief from air attack, was
now falling, but astern of Ohio and her little group of
protectors, the merchantman Dorset had ended her
brave struggle to reach Malta. Hit by three more bombs,
she settled down slowly by the head. Not many minutes
after her crew had abandoned her, she sank. Dorset's
escort, the destroyer Bramham, picked up the survivors,
and then joined the fight to save Ohio.

There now came a parting of the ways for Ohio's crew.
Chief Engineer Wyld, Chief Officer Gray, and Third
Mate Stephen, with some thirty of the crew, had gone
aboard launch 168. They took it in turn to smoke
thirteen cigarettes contributed by Pumpman Collins,
the only ones remaining amongst them, then all dropped
off into a dreamless sleep. When they awoke they were
in Malta. The launch had developed an engine defect
and had been ordered to return to the Island. Ashore
they settled down to what seemed the greatest feed of
their life – tinned herrings, dry bread and tea. They were
safe, yet every man felt vaguely cheated. Collins
expressed it like this: 'Don't know what you chaps
think, but I wish we could have stood by the old bitch
to the end,' he said. The others nodded and murmured
agreement.

Meanwhile, the other launch had put the critically
injured gunner and Captain Mason aboard Penn. The
tanker's master was immediately called for a conference
with Lieutenant-Commander Swain, captain of Penn.

'Do you think she'll last?' he asked, as Mason reached
the bridge.

Mason shook his head: 'Difficult to say, sir,' he
replied. 'The engine-room and after end are flooding but
the forward end is holding its buoyancy. She'll have to

break her back if that goes on. Still, we've got to get some of that oil to Malta if we can.'

Lieutenant-Commander Swain nodded: 'We'll do everything we can. But you'd better get some sleep, Captain. You look all in.'

'I suppose you're right,' said Mason, with a grin. 'We've had a fairly busy day, you know.'

While Mason at last found sleep in a corner of the ward-room, the captains of *Penn* and *Rye* had a parley. A new plan was made. A small party from *Penn*, under the leadership of Lieutenant George Marten, the executive officer, went aboard the tanker. *Rye* took the towing position ahead, securing the chain cable previously slipped by *Penn*. *Penn* made fast astern of the tanker, acting as rear tug to keep *Ohio* from swinging. Meanwhile, *Bramham* circled the group, watching for submarines.

Slowly they worked up speed and not long after midnight had reached four and a half knots. At one o'clock, however, *Rye* decided to attempt a further increase of speed. It was too much. The tanker took charge and careered to port, out of control. Before the towlines could be cast off, both had snapped.

Lieutenant-Commander Swain was now in a quandary. In the pitch dark a renewal of the tow would be difficult, moreover, the method they had been using plainly would not work. While some new means of getting the tanker moving were being sought, *Bramham* signalled the suggestion that attempts should be made to move the tanker by towing alongside. This scheme was immediately adopted and Swain began the delicate manœuvre of laying *Penn* alongside the damaged tanker in the dark.

With engines scarcely turning over, the destroyer glided up to the tanker. As the two ships came together, the jagged rent in the derelict's side grated ominously on *Penn*'s plates despite the fenders over her sides.

The ships were made fast and Swain rang down for

slow ahead. The grinding and grating increased, but *Ohio* remained stationary. The destroyer tried full speed, but it soon became apparent that the tanker was too heavy to be moved by a single destroyer. Moreover, the alarming noises from between the two ships threatened serious damage if this method was continued. Commander Swain rang *Penn*'s engines to stop.

Since the destroyer had gone alongside *Ohio* a steady stream of men had been passing between the two ships. Despite their own ordeal, the American survivors from *Santa Elisa* could not resist a souvenir hunt. Pieces of crashed aircraft, shell splinters, bullets and mangled pieces of metal from *Ohio*'s own wounds were all quickly snapped up. Many of *Penn*'s crew were also busy. Some items in the magnificent stores aboard the American tanker were rare aboard His Majesty's ships at that time. Also the tanker had a well-stocked NAAFI. No one believed *Ohio* would last the night and there seemed to be no harm in 'liberating' such valuable supplies from the hungry sea. When Captain Mason awoke next morning he saw his own typewriter installed on *Penn*'s ward-room table.

Finally, Commander Swain decided that further attempts at towing in the darkness were hopeless. *Penn* cast off, and once more the tanker was alone. Low in the water, her engine-room flooded and groaning now with every movement of the Mediterranean as the sinking after-part placed more and more strain on the torpedo damage, the end seemed near. Malta was still more than sixty miles away.

To the westward, Admiral Burrough's Force X was rounding Cape Bon at twenty-one knots on their voyage back to Gibraltar. Meanwhile, *Ledbury*, returning from her search for *Manchester*, was steaming at full speed to the aid of *Ohio*. As darkness began to tinge with the pink of dawn, they had arrived at the estimated position of the tanker, but could find no sign of her. A little later

Commander Hill sighted gunfire ahead. It was *Ohio*'s
escort beating off the first snoopers of the day.

As *Ledbury* approached in the gaining daylight, her
crew sighted *Ohio*. She was lying deep in the water now,
down by the stern; the line of the deck seemed to be
decidedly bent.

Hill turned to Hollins, his number one: 'It looks as
though we're too late,' he said.

CHAPTER FIFTEEN

The Long Tow

Penn to Senior Officer Mine-sweepers:
14/8/42 0755 POSITION 36 DEGREES 2 MINUTES
NORTH 013 DEGREES 10 MINUTES EAST RYE
BRAMHAM AND MLS IN COMPANY STOP OHIO DEEPLY
DAMAGED WITHOUT STEERING WILL NOT TOW STOP
RYE TRYING AGAIN AND WILL CONTINUE TO TRY
MESSAGE ENDS

While the little fleet of ships surrounding *Ohio* were preparing to make further attempts to tow after a night of failure, Captain Mason stood on an oil drum on the low stern of *Penn*. A few of *Ohio*'s crew, who had awakened, stood round him. On a grating rigged by one of the entry ports lay a tightly-sewn bundle of canvas. It contained the body of Gunner Brown, now ready for burial at sea. He had died during the night.

Mason took off his steel helmet and the men standing round him followed suit. Unhurriedly, he began reading the burial service. Some of *Penn*'s ratings, paying out a steel hawser, paused in their work, took off their tin hats and also stood silent with their heads bowed.

'We therefore commit his body to the deep.'

Bosun Thacker of *Ohio* tipped the grating. The swathed body slipped into the sea. A swirl of water, a few bubbles, and it was gone.

'. . . according to the mighty working, whereby He is able to subdue all things to Himself.' Mason put on his tin hat, got down from the oil drum and looked over the side. It seemed an age since the ventilator had fallen, years and years since they had passed Gibraltar. Now the dawn of another day was breaking, and there was work to do. He shook the tiredness off him and went to report to the captain of *Penn*.

During the night Commander Swain had tried once more to tow the tanker with her own 10-inch manilla, but this too, had failed.

As Mason reached the bridge, the commander had just received a message from *Ledbury*: 'May we help?' Commander Swain turned to his Chief Yeoman: 'Send "For goodness sake, yes, we need it" to *Ledbury*,' he said. Then, turning to Mason: 'Well, Captain, we're going to have another try. We've got more ships now. But I don't like the looks of your tanker.'

Mason gazed at *Ohio*, carefully measuring levels. 'I doubt if she's got much more than three or four foot free-board,' he said. 'But tankers are funny things. This one's really tough. She might stay afloat.'

The two men watched as *Rye* passed the end of her 300 fathoms of sweep wire to the small naval party aboard the tanker. Meanwhile, *Ledbury* was making fast astern of her so that when the tow began they would have more control over the tendency of the derelict to sheer.

Once more *Rye* got the tanker moving, and *Ledbury*, going astern, tried to keep her straight; but she pulled too hard and both tows parted.

On *Penn*'s bridge Captain Mason commented: 'If they try that too often they'll pull the ship in half. She's only hanging on amidships with about half her keel.'

Ledbury cautiously approached the port side of *Ohio* and made fast alongside. She immediately put aboard a small party of men under the gunner, Charles Musham, and the men busied themselves on the tanker's fo'c'sle, passing down a big towing hawser to *Ledbury*. The most active man amongst them was Cook, the bosun of *Melbourne Star*. Despite his dreadful experiences in the blazing grave of *Waimarama*, and nearly two hours in the sea waiting to be picked up, the bosun was back on duty, a mine of energy and practical seamanship.

Other survivors of the merchantmen were also anxious to bear a hand, amongst them the American third officer of *Santa Elisa* Frederick Larsen. He went to Commander Hill and asked if he could take a party aboard *Ohio* to repair and man one of the anti-aircraft guns. *Ledbury*'s captain gladly accepted the offer. Many of his own crew had had no sleep for three days and it was as much as they could do to cope with the problems aboard the destroyer.

Larsen, with Cadet Dale and three of the British gunners from *Santa Elisa* then boarded the tanker and at once set to work clearing the debris of the ventilator from the Bofors gun, and within half an hour they were ready to meet the next air attack, which, to judge by the activity of snooping aircraft, could be expected at any time.

None of these men, in spite of their previous experiences, seemed to worry about the fact that *Ohio* now had no lifeboats, was sinking and would be a certain target for every enemy attacker.

Ledbury, her tow secured, now sheered off, and, despite the fact that she was only alongside about five minutes, unofficial boarding parties 'acquired' one large typewriter, a number of telephones of which the destroyer had much need, two Oerlikon cannons and twelve magazines, besides a variety of smaller articles including a fine megaphone with SS *Ohio* stamped on it.

Meanwhile, *Rye* had again begun to tow *Ohio* with *Ledbury* acting as stern tug. With less pull from *Ledbury*, a fair speed was maintained, but, once again, steering proved impossible. The shattered tanker was pointing more often in any direction except towards Malta.

Clearly, a stabilizing factor was needed, and Commander Swain edged *Penn* into the starboard side of *Ohio*, and made fast alongside her.

As soon as this manœuvre had been completed, two more parties went aboard the stricken tanker. One was led by *Penn*'s engineer officer, Lieutenant-Commander John Sweall, RN, who had orders to try to improve *Ohio*'s buoyancy.

The other consisted of Captain Mason who, with Commander Swain's permission, went to examine his ship with eight members of *Ohio*'s crew.

Mason began by sounding all the tanks and he found the picture better than might have been expected. Empty tanks and holds were still intact and dry, though kerosene was still overflowing from the port tanks where the lids had been buckled by torpedo explosion. Evidently, the chief doubt was whether the keel plate could hold *Ohio* together or not. With the forward part of the tanker buoyant and the stern sinking, an intolerable strain had been placed on the amidships section, rent as it was, right across and almost down to the bottom.

Meanwhile, Commander Sweall had examined the tanker's compressed air system to see if it could be used to increase the buoyancy of the tanks which were not leaking or which could be sealed. So great had been the battering that the tanker had received during days of attack, that scarcely a foot of compressed air-line was undamaged, and it was plainly out of the question to attempt to use it. He, therefore, sent to the destroyer for portable pumps, and these were brought aboard and set to work pumping the water out of the engine-room.

Mason and Sweall had a hasty conference.

'The ship is pretty sound except for the amidships section,' said Mason. 'But unless we can check the flooding aft she's bound to break her back. Do you think you can hold the water with your pumps?'

Commander Sweall shook his head: 'It's difficult to say. If there's no further damage she might hold up.' He did a quick calculation: 'As far as I can see she's still making about six inches an hour in the engine-room, and we're doing the best we can.'

Commander Swain passed the master's report to Commander Jerome in *Speedy* who was now the senior officer. He had returned with the fleet mine-sweepers *Speedy*, *Hebe* and *Hythe* to help with the tow and to form a protective screen.

Aboard *Ohio*, Gunner Musham, organizing the manning of the guns, was swearing quietly under his breath:

'Some bastard has pinched all the Oerlikon gun sights,' he muttered.

Nevertheless, he placed himself behind one of the sightless Oerlikons and saw with satisfaction that ammunition parties were at the ready.

Behind the Bofors gun, the American, Larsen, hummed gently to himself: 'Sister Anne, Sister Anne, can you see anyone coming?'

Then as *Ledbury* was stopped, the wire hawser she had made fast to the stern of the tanker hung down in a great bight between the two ships. It was found to be resting on her starboard propeller, threatening to become foul of it as soon as she got under way. After a short flap, the danger was averted. *Ledbury* went ahead slowly on her port propeller and the hawser was eased out of harm's way.

Rye and *Bramham* slowly got under way again with *Ledbury* acting as a rudder. Gradually working up speed, they soon had the tanker crabbing through the water at more than six knots. The tendency to sheer had been overcome, and success at last seemed to be within their grasp.

Now, however, when hopes had risen high, and when it seemed that the vital cargo could at last be brought to Malta, the drone of many bombers' engines filled the air. It was plain that the Axis were making another attempt to finish off the tanker. At 10.45 the first wave of dive-bombers could be seen coming in to attack. The dark shapes of six Junkers 88s came streaking over the water towards *Ohio*. All the guns opened up together. Gunner Musham, without sights to his guns, sprayed the oncoming formation hosepipe fashion. The leading aircraft began to stream black smoke, broke formation, and dived into the sea at nearly 300 miles an hour, sending up a great column of spray. The other aircraft, daunted by the thick, accurate barrage, dropped their bombs and turned aside too early. Only one oil bomb crashed close to the bows of *Ohio*, showering her prow with black burning liquid.

Three more echelons of German planes could now be seen approaching, but help was at hand. Sixteen Spitfires of 249 and 229 Squadrons from Malta, despite lack of R/T direction, and with no warning from radar of the impending attack, had sighted the enemy. Diving in from 6,000 feet, they attacked the Junkers 88s from ahead. The first enemy formation wavered and broke. Half the Spitfires pressed on to attack the two following flights while the other half turned sharply and got in among the disorganized German aircraft. Two black bombers fell out of the air flaming. The second flight of Junkers also broke as the Spitfires flashed through them. Dog-fights had now developed all over the sky, but part of the third German formation pressed on towards the ships. One section of Spitfires broke away from the general engagement and pursued it. It was a question of whether the bombers could reach the tanker before they were overtaken by the Spitfires. The British planes closed in, their guns firing. Three of the German aircraft began to jink, their bombing fatally interrupted. A single Junkers 88 held its course, and a 1,000-pound bomb came hurtling down towards *Ohio*.

It landed directly in the wake of the tanker, and she was flung violently forward, parting *Rye*'s tow. The stern plates buckled, and the dark waters gushed in through a great hole.

Meanwhile, the only other straggler from the convoy left afloat, the battered *Brisbane Star*, was sailing proudly towards the Grand Harbour under her own

steam, protected from above by a strong escort of Beaufighters and Spitfires.

Since his exchange with the signal station at Hammamet, her master, Captain Riley, had passed safely
through many vicissitudes.

No attempt had been made to stop him as he sailed
on down the Gulf of Hammamet until after several
hours' steaming the lookout sighted a U-boat out to sea.
There followed a game of hide-and-seek among the
tricky shallows which border this part of the Tunisian
coast. The situation was a strange one, for the U-boat
dared not attack her in French territorial waters. He had
been specifically warned not to do this by the Axis High
Command. At the same time, Captain Riley knew that
it was only a matter of time before he would be stopped
by the French authorities. Yet he dare not cut out into
the open sea and set course for Malta. The U-boat would
at once have torpedoed him. The English captain therefore continued to hug the shore while the U-boat cruised
slowly along, parallel with him and just outside
territorial waters.

At first it seemed as though luck was with the
merchantman. There had been no further air attack and
now the sun was low in the sky and soon, hidden by
darkness, she would stand a good chance of being able
to evade the U-boat.

At five o'clock, however, the lookouts reported a
small vessel putting out from Monastir Bay. As she
approached, she broke out the French Tricolour, and
Captain Riley realized that this was a French patrol boat
and that the game was probably up. The French Ensign
was followed by a signal to 'Heave to.' Captain Riley
altered course away from the patrol boat and called for
an Aldis signalling lamp. He proceeded to flash a series
of messages which were far too fast to be decipherable.
The patrol vessel once again hoisted the signal to 'Heave
to.' Captain Riley once again flashed a series of inde-
cipherable dots and dashes. As the sun sank lower the

tragi-comedy proceeded. Every time the Frenchman signalled, Captain Riley turned his ship away and sent back an unintelligible signal. Finally, long before it got dark, the Frenchman's patience was exhausted and the warning shot fired across *Brisbane Star*'s bows came unpleasantly close. The captain had no option but to heave to.

Two French officers then boarded the merchantman. Both saluted the captain punctiliously and he, with courtesy equal to their own, bowed them into the captain's cabin.

Now that all else had failed, this tall, good-looking Irishman meant to try the effect of blarney as a last resort.

The Frenchman came straight to the point: 'I regret, Monsieur, that you will have to follow us to port. You and the crew must be interned,' he said.

'But surely, Captain,' said Riley, with a charming smile, 'you realize that that is impossible for me.' He rummaged in a locker and brought out a bottle of whisky. 'I regret, my friends, that I cannot offer you wine. It is not easy to get, now your charming country is inaccessible to us. Perhaps the wine of Scotland would please you?'

The conversation proceeded pleasantly. Half an hour later the two Frenchmen returned on deck with the captain, laughing and chatting gaily. An injured crew member of *Brisbane Star* was put in the boat to be taken to hospital. Both French officers shook hands enthusiastically, wishing the captain 'Bon Voyage.' Then, in the gathering night, the Frenchmen sailed back to port while *Brisbane Star* proceeded on her voyage.

Now that the French had been pacified, Captain Riley set himself to outwit the U-boat. With brilliant navigation, he twisted and turned amongst the inshore shoals until he rightly judged that he had thrown his would-be attacker off the scent; then, mustering no more than eight knots, *Brisbane Star* headed out to sea and on towards Malta.

Next day she was escorted into Grand Harbour, down by the head with her forward holds badly flooded but still preserving most of her cargo intact.

All the surviving ships had now reached Malta safely, except *Ohio* and her devoted protectors.

Force X, retiring to the west, weathered a series of dive-bombing attacks, but these appeared to be desultory as though the Axis forces were tiring at last. Making twenty-five knots they rejoined Admiral Syfret's force at dusk on the 14th and returned to Gibraltar.

Yet, Malta's fate still depended upon *Ohio*. Unless her cargo could be saved, all the effort and loss of 'Operation Pedestal' had been in vain.

CHAPTER SIXTEEN

Proud to Have Met You

Ohio was sinking slowly not much more than forty-five miles west of Malta, which she had been sent to save. As if to prove how much lower in the water she had become, one of the gunners walking aft, leant over the side and drew a bucket of water to cool off one of the gun barrels before changing it. The ship had little more than two feet of free-board left.

From her decks came the steady beat of portable pumps struggling to check the water in the engine-room, but when Captain Mason and Commander Sweall peered down the companionway, the marks they had made an hour earlier at water level were no longer visible. Slowly but inexorably they were losing the battle to maintain the tanker's buoyancy.

The danger from the air was receding and a whole circus of Malta Spitfires now weaved and circled above the little convoy of ships; but, grouped as they were about the unmanœuvrable 30,000 tons of deadweight represented by the derelict tanker, all were sitting targets for the first U-boat which could approach unobserved. Moreover, even if the tanker stayed afloat, night would come before they reached safety. It was unlikely that the Axis would miss the opportunity then of attacking so valuable a target with the E-boats which had already struck at the convoy in darkness off the Tunisian coast with such devastating results.

Nevertheless, these seemed minor details in the race for time which faced Commander Jerome if he was to save *Ohio* and relieve Malta. The tanker's life at sea was clearly to be measured in hours – no one knew how few. It was with the certainty that she must sink, perhaps at any minute, that he began to reorganize the tow, dislocated by the Axis air attack.

In this attempt to get the tanker moving again, a less tangible barrier loomed like a spectre denying them final passage to Malta. When all depended on the speed of their action, the men of the little rescue fleet were rapidly running down, like engines progressively starved of fuel. To most of them sleep had now become as a distant view of paradise. For days they had conquered sleep or given way to it only in small, disturbed snatches, and now the demands of their tired bodies, shaken by the drumming of the barrage, drenched with sea water, and worn by the incessant call to action, could scarcely be resisted. Fingers fumbled, co-ordination was lost and judgement failed. Determination and grit began to dissolve into the wavering motifs of a dream.

Ledbury, still secured to *Ohio* by a heavy wire, had been pulled round by the yawing tanker and had ended up alongside *Penn*, facing the wrong way. *Rye* was ordered to tow from ahead, and came alongside to take *Ledbury*'s end of the wire. Lieutenant Hollins, driving himself and his tired men, had the tow quickly passed, but aboard *Rye*, too, lack of sleep and strain were beginning to overcome seamanship. Someone made fast the wire with a slippery hitch and, as soon as the destroyer went ahead and the strain came on, the cable snaked through the towing bitts and splashed into the water. Soon it was hanging straight down from *Ohio*'s bows into the depths. There was no question of hauling it aboard the tanker. Without power for the winches it would have taken 100 fresh men to carry out such a heavy job. There was nothing to do but slip it, as the trailing end would have collected any moored mines in the vicinity, as soon as the derelict was got under way again.

Commander Jerome, who with the crew of *Speedy* was less troubled with the deadening effects of tiredness, for they had only recently sailed from Malta, saw that any further complicated patterns for towing the tanker were likely to degenerate into a series of frustrating errors. Somehow an easier method of moving her had to be found.

After a quick analysis of possible means, he decided that despite the danger of damage from the sharp metal edges of *Ohio*'s torpedo hole, they would have to try to tow the tanker with a destroyer made fast on either side. This would tend to offset the drag and also act as something of a 'splint' for the broken and dangerously strained amidships section of the derelict. *Bramham* was immediately ordered to make fast to port while *Penn* remained coupled to the starboard side.

As the *Bramham* moved in, her number one, Lieutenant the Marquess of Milford Haven, OBE, RN, was working marvels with the sleep-soggy men. Additional fenders to guard the destroyer's sides were speedily improvised and steel wires made ready, so that the destroyer was secured to the tanker within a few minutes of going alongside, and all was ready for another attempt to tow.

Slowly the destroyers began to get under way. White water creamed behind their sterns. The cables creaked, slipped and bit on the bollards. The amidships section of *Ohio* groaned and the working of the damaged plates could be heard harshly grating. Yet the tanker began to move and to gather speed.

As she did so, Mason anxiously gazed into the torpedo rent in the pump-room. They had reached five knots and the 'old girl' was still holding together. As the speed increased a little more, a rending, tearing sound began to murmur through the bones of the ship. He could feel and hear that she would not stand much more.

He hailed *Penn*'s captain: 'I don't think she'll take any more speed, sir. Can you keep it at that?' he shouted. Commander Swain nodded and gave an order to his number one.

The speed was held at five knots, a steady five knots

now in the direction of Malta, but in the engine-room of the battered tanker water swirled over the marks scratched on the walls of the companionway and the gentle swell of the calm Mediterranean now washed over the deck amidships.

Just past midday, when hopes were beginning to rise again, one of *Bramham*'s wires parted with a crack. The destroyer sprang away from the tanker's side and with *Penn* manœuvring desperately with her engines to keep the derelict straight, the tow came to a sudden stop.

The men of *Bramham* looked woodenly at the parted tow. It seemed impossible to go through the effort of making fast again. Milford Haven fought down tiredness. In an instant he was down among the men again, lending a hand himself, joking, encouraging. Like sleepwalkers the ratings responded to his driving spirit, the broken wire was cast off and a new one run out, the fenders were manned, and once more *Bramham* glided alongside the tanker. Somehow they made fast again, slower this time, for the naval party aboard *Ohio* were also heavy with sleep and even that giant of energy, *Melbourne Star*'s bosun, moved wearily with reluctant limbs; but the job was done somehow, and within half an hour *Ohio* was once more moving through the water at five knots.

The men were finally beginning to give way to the imperative need for rest. Gunners slumped behind their guns staring glassily at nothing, though they remained at their posts they were asleep. It was doubtful whether they could have wakened in time to fight off another air attack. All about the ship men lay, sat or leaned in awkward, unnatural attitudes, either asleep or on the edge of sleep. If the tow parted once more, it seemed doubtful if enough men could be found fit to secure it again. Helmsmen clung to the wheels for support and the captains and officers were blinking sleep away in desperate efforts to concentrate.

The afternoon wore on, and then through the haze

ahead the tired eyes of the lookouts sighted a dim blue blotch of land, the high cliffs of Dingli – Malta.

The men gathered themselves for another effort, for here along the south-west coast of the Island the enemy submarines would probably be waiting. *Ledbury* and *Speedy* began circling *Ohio* and her three lined consorts. Every twenty minutes *Ledbury* dropped a depth-charge hoping to scare any lurking submarine away or at least to discourage it from surfacing and taking sights on so perfect a target.

After several of these warning explosions had detonated, a new danger presented itself. Shock waves from the depth-charges were shaking *Ohio*. Captain Mason and Commander Sweall, now almost constantly watching the damaged pump-room saw that the rent was gradually opening. Then one of the underwater disturbances was followed by a loud and ominous crack. Mason quickly informed *Penn*'s captain and a message was flashed on the signalling lamp to *Ledbury*: 'Stop depth-charging. The shock is sinking the tanker.' This was greeted by groans from the more wakeful. After all that effort and within sight of their goal, surely they were not going to lose *Ohio* now?

The light was waning slowly. As the towing destroyers forged on, the coastline of Malta became plainer and they were approaching Filfla, the tiny rocky islet five miles to the south-west of the Island. Here it was necessary to alter course to port to make the entrance to the swept channel in the mine-fields off Delimara Point. This was a tricky operation as it placed a heavy strain on the towing wires. There was also considerable anxiety over imparting any lateral strain to *Ohio*. The two halves of the tanker on either side of the torpedo gash amidships were held together by only a few plates. At a given signal, *Penn* increased speed slightly while *Bramham* slowed. For nearly a minute the wires held and the derelict tanker began to turn to port. Then a slight swell rocked the ships and with loud reports the towing wires parted.

Once more the officers succeeded in rousing the men and the now laborious business of making fast was begun all over again. At this stage, an old paddle-wheeler naval tug named *Robert* was sighted approaching from Malta.

In her was the King's Harbour Master who took charge of the tow. The tug was secured to *Ohio* and, as she went ahead, the tanker began to swing to port dragging her as easily as if she had been a cork. It soon became evident that unless her crew could slip the tow she would collide with *Penn*. A party struggled hard to unshackle the pin which held the hawser, but whether, as her captain maintained later, there was too much strain on to do so or whether her crew had omitted to grease the pin as some suspected, her stern drove relentlessly into *Penn*, holing the destroyer in the ward-room, fortunately above the waterline. For some minutes the air was blue with the comments of *Penn*'s captain.

After this episode, in which precious time was wasted, *Robert* was sent back to Malta and the destroyers ranged up again on either side of the tanker. By sheer force of spirit, the nightmare of making fast was accomplished and *Ohio*, embraced on either side, began to move onwards, while the mine-sweepers searched the channel ahead.

At Malta, anxiety for *Ohio* and for her cargo, upon which the survival of the Island rested as if on a sharp knife edge, had reached a high pitch. Coastal defences had been alerted, lookout stations and the radar-room scanned the seas with desperate urgency for signs of enemy activity. In the combined operations room, chiefs of staff waited tensely for news, as the tanker and her escorts crawled round the darkening extremity of the Island. Night was succeeding the dusk when a radar plot of a submarine was confirmed following the slowly-moving derelict on the surface.

Colonel C. J. White of the Royal Artillery ordered his men to go into action with the coastal batteries. Search-lights began to finger the calm waters and men strained their eyes to pick out the tiny silhouette of the submar-ine, while Commander Jerome, informed of the danger by wireless, ordered all guns to readiness.

Suddenly a strong beam of light found and held the tanker and her two consorts in dazzling brilliance. Readily seen for miles and her defenders blinded by the searchlight, the tanker was a sitting target for the submarine.

'For God's sake don't show me up,' Jerome signalled. Lights winked desperately from the destroyers warning the soldiers to turn off the light. Then the searchlight went out. In the little fleet, the men waited tensely for their night sight to return, conscious that at any moment an unseen torpedo might rip into one of the ships. For the damage had been done and if the enemy submarine was anywhere in the vicinity she must have sighted them.

Meanwhile, *Hebe* sighted something and opened fire. The shell passed over one of the coastal batteries and the gunners, taking the mine-sweepers for an enemy, were about to open fire too. Fortunately, their central control stopped them in time. The coastal defences which had unknowingly jeopardized the whole rescue operation, were soon to remove the danger, however. Higher up the coast, another searchlight picked out the U-boat speeding towards the convoy on the surface. Immediately, the 9·2-inch coastal guns opened up and shots were observed falling round the shadowy conning tower. The submarine hurriedly submerged and was not seen again.

Then a new danger, greater than the other, material-ized. Once again, radar men scanning the seas on the north side of the Island, picked up a number of small fast-moving plots. There could be only one interpret-ation of these 'blips' on the radar screens. A flotilla of E-boats was steaming down the north-east coast of

Malta to intercept the tanker as she came up the east
coast of the Island to make Valletta. The rescue fleet
and all shore stations were once again alerted.

Colonel White had, however, already worked out a
plan to counter just such a situation. As the enemy
approached the coast they were greeted by a heavy
barrage from the coastal batteries firing on the radar
plots. Then, ahead of them, the beam of a strong searchlight was exposed in the path they would have to take
to close Ohio and her protectors. If they steamed into
the beam, they would be subjected to accurate visual
fire from the coastal batteries and if they succeeded in
passing through it they would still be a silhouetted
target for the British MLs which were now in line
abreast ahead of the tanker and destroyers preparing to
meet the attack.

The E-boats held their course. Aboard Ohio and her
consorts, the men could hear the firing which came
perceptibly closer as new coastal batteries opened up to
engage the approaching enemy ships. The tired naval
gunners again stood by for action. The radar scanners
watched the two groups of ships and the diminishing
distance between them. Would the enemy risk a bold
dash across the wide beam of the fighting light? It was a
tense moment, because no one could be certain that the
full force of an attack could be successfully countered.
Once the E-boats got among the little fleet, hampered as
it was with the unmanœuvrable derelict, and in darkness, some of the enemy ships would no doubt be able
to carry out an attack on the tanker. In her precarious
state of buoyancy, even the distant concussion of an
exploding torpedo might be sufficient to send her to the
bottom.

The plot of the E-boats crept slowly towards the area
of water which the scanners knew was illuminated.
Suddenly, the little blobs of light faded. The E-boats
were turning. Then, as they brightened again, it could

be seen that they were travelling in the opposite direction. Faced with the certainty of accurate fire from the coastal batteries as he passed through the brightly-lit corridor of sea, the E-boat flotilla commander decided not to take the risk and gave the order to retire. The defenders were able to breathe again.

Ohio and her escorts now approached a difficult corner in the swept channel where it rounded Zonkar Point and made a sharp turn to the north-west. With only a matter of a few cables-length separating him from mine-fields on either side, Commander Jerome knew that there would be considerable danger here to both the tanker and her towing destroyers.

When half the turn had been made, the tanker began to take charge. Despite the efforts of *Penn* and *Bramham*, she swung slowly but inexorably towards the mine-field and the destroyers were forced to halt progress altogether. They then lay stopped, the bows of the tanker pointing towards the side of the channel. All three ships were slowly drifting towards the mine-field.

An emergency signal was made for *Ledbury* to take them in tow ahead and attempt to draw them away from the disaster which now lay not more than 50 yards distant. The destroyer went alongside and passed her faithful 6-inch manilla to *Ohio*. Then began half an hour's struggle to edge the tanker away from the mine-field. As *Ledbury* towed, the two MLs assisted by pushing against her bows and keeping her going in the right direction. As they grated down *Ledbury*'s side, agonizing cries from the destroyer's sick bay echoed across the water adding horror to the anxiety of the situation. The badly burned survivors of *Waimarama* were now suffering from secondary shock and the noises on the ship's hull had awakened them. They kept screaming and shouting that the ship was being blown up.

A grey light began to appear in the east and the longed-for dawn was at hand. But light brought with it the danger of renewed air attacks, and an overcast sky which began to be visible seemed ideal for sneak raiders. The gunners, rested now despite the alarms of the night, anxiously peered at the breaks in the cloud, fingering their triggers.

At 6 a.m., with *Ohio* still hovering on the edge of the mine-field, the situation was eased by the arrival of the Malta tugs. With the destroyers still linked on either side of the tanker, two of these sturdy little ships made fast ahead and astern and the tanker was soon proceeding up the channel to the Grand Harbour entrance.

There a fabulous welcome awaited them. On the ramparts above the wreck-strewn harbour, on the Baracca, at St Angelo and Senglea, great crowds of Maltese men and women waved and cheered and a brass band on the end of the mole was giving a spirited rendering of *Rule Britannia*.

Captain Mason, however, standing at the salute on the battered bridge of *Ohio*, could spare no moment's thought for the pride of bringing his wounded ship to port. The tanker's main deck was now freely washed by the sea. The tortured plates amidships creaked and groaned alarmingly with every movement, and the captain knew that at any moment, the epic fight of *Ohio* might end with the tanker at the bottom of the Grand Harbour.

As the destroyers cast off, *Penn*'s captain called across to Mason. 'Just got this message from Admiral Burrough, with Force X,' he said. 'It reads: "To *Ohio* stop I'm proud to have met you message ends." That goes for us too.'

Mason smiled wanly: 'We're here thanks to you chaps. But it isn't over yet. This poor old hooker hasn't got many minutes now. I hope to God she lasts long enough.'

The tugs dragged the derelict slowly towards the quays. There, waiting, was the tanker's chief engineer, Jimmy Wyld, Gray, the first officer, and the other crew members who had been brought to Malta in the damaged ML. Wyld had spent several hours with the Dockyard Superintendent, Rear-Admiral Mackenzie, discussing the difficult technical problem of discharging the tanker. All was prepared to reap the priceless harvest of oil and kerosene without a moment's delay.

Now, as Wyld watched *Ohio*'s slow approach, he realized how close might be the time margin for discharging the tanker, bereft of all her power pumping equipment.

'Look at that free-board,' he said to Gray. 'I can't think how she stays afloat. We'll have to get a move on.'

Slowly *Ohio* drew in alongside *Plumleaf*, an auxiliary tanker lying bombed and sunk by the quayside, her upperworks showing. A hundred willing pairs of hands helped to make her fast. At the same time another fleet auxiliary, *Boxall*, secured on the seaward side.

Wyld boarded the tanker and wrung Mason's hand warmly: 'Good show, lad. You've made it.'

Now that the moment for action was passed, a great wave of tiredness surged over the captain. Now he had to sleep.

'See to her, Jimmy,' he mumbled. 'I must get ashore.' Like a man in a dream he stumbled towards the ship's side followed by the other members of the crew who had brought the tanker in.

Pipes were now hauled aboard and, superintended by Wyld, emergency salvage pumps began to discharge the kerosene. At the same time *Boxall* began to pump the 10,000 tons of fuel oil into her own tanks.

As the tanker's holds were pumped out and the forward end of the ship lightened, it became plain that she would soon break her back, for the waterlogged after-end continued to sink. There was a hurried conference of experts, for a real danger still existed that they might lose the remainder of the oil. If the ship broke in half, the lighter half might easily capsize. They decided to flood the tanks with sea water as the oil was removed.

In this way the oil floated on top and could easily be removed by the pumps as the water flowed in and acted as ballast.

As the oil flowed out, *Ohio* sank lower and lower in the water. The last gallon left her and simultaneously her keel settled gently on the bottom. She had found rest at last.

On the bridge, which with the poop now alone remained above water, Buddle, the second engineer, saw a Maltese stevedore idly scraping the oxidation away in flakes from the twisted rail. Suddenly, an unreasoning anger took possession of him.

'Leave it alone,' he roared. 'Don't you think the poor old cow's suffered enough?'

EPILOGUE

One fine September morning, four years later, early
risers on the quays of the Grand Harbour, Malta, were
treated to an unusual spectacle. Two busy posses of tugs
were passing through the harbour entrance making for
the calm blue sea beyond.

They carried with them two strange, rust-streaked
boxes of metal; and, from the larger of the two, with its
bridgework still intact and its graceful schooner bow,
some of the watchers might have inferred that the
remnant of a war-damaged tanker was being taken to
sea in two halves.

At this date, the 19 September 1946, with the war
over more than a year and more than two since the
Island had seen any enemy action, it is unlikely that her
name would have meant very much to them.

Someone with a retentive memory might have haz-
arded: 'Wasn't that the tanker that brought the oil in?
You remember . . . when we had almost had it in August
1942.'

Another might have replied: 'Well, perhaps it is. What
were we saying before that . . .?'

The war was over. No one likes to remember times of
starvation, death and danger. And then so much had
happened. The invasion of Italy, the surrender of the
Italian fleet at Valletta, the invasion of the Continent,
the fall of Hitler, VE Day. Then the eclipse of the Rising
Sun, the atom bomb and VJ Day – the war's end.

The day they cheered *Ohio* into the same harbour was
so long ago and so was the award of the George Cross to
Captain Dudley Mason. Few now remembered the epic
of 'Operation Pedestal', the many awards for heroism
which followed it – and the casualty list. Who can blame

them? That was their yesterday and their tomorrow held
the problems of peace not those of war.

The ship which had saved Malta and perhaps the free
world, had herself become a familiar part of the harbour
scenery, and familiarity had soon shorn her of her heroic
trappings. Not long after her precious cargo had been
discharged, she had been hauled away and had later
broken in half at her moorings.

Some efforts were made at repair. The bulkheads of
the two halves were shored and sealed watertight; but it
had proved impossible to provide the skilled techniques
for joining the ship together locally, and the expense of
towing the two halves to Gibraltar or Alexandria was
too great to justify.

For a time the dismembered ship was used for a store.
Then, towards the end of the war, she was fitted out to
house Yugoslav troops. Now, even these services were
no longer required in peacetime and the hulks had
become a nuisance in the busy waterway.

The two halves of Ohio passed through the harbour
entrance and what remained of this ship of destiny felt
once more the surge of the open sea.

Steering north-eastward over the tail of St George's
Shoals, over the site of the old mine-field, the tugs
headed for deep water, towards the lithe shape of a
destroyer, shining in peacetime paint and waiting for
them.

Ten miles from Malta they cast off the tow and the
two halves of Ohio were alone again on the deep,
heaving gently in the swell.

Aboard the destroyer, the number one rubbed his
hands with satisfaction and remarked to the captain:
'This will make a useful shoot, sir. The men can do with
it.' By this time, there were men aboard who had not
seen a shot fired in anger, and any suitable opportunity
for gunnery practice was welcome to the first lieutenant.

'Load armour piercing,' the gunnery officer ordered.
'Fire!'

A forward gun spat flame and smoke and the report echoed across the sea.

'Over,' remarked the gunnery officer conversationally and began to bracket. Soon the guns were registering on the two halves of the tanker, and the rear portion, weakened by the battering it had received from Axis airmen long before, soon disappeared from sight.

Shell after shell pumped into the buoyant forepart of the tanker. 'Can't think why she won't sink,' said number one. 'Must have been a tough old ship. In some convoy or other, wasn't she?'

The bridgework had been blasted away, the foremast had fallen, and now the shored-up amidships section, where the torpedo had struck, caved in. Slowly the forward half also sank and the grateful bows reared up like a finger pointing to heaven. Then she was gone, and seventy-five fathoms below the blue water of the Mediterranean the rippled sands received the brave bones of *Ohio*.

'Cease fire,' the captain ordered. 'Carry on, Number One.'

There were no fine words for this great ship, no flowers, no wreaths bobbing on the water. Only the laurel of fame not soon to die.

BIBLIOGRAPHY

PRINCIPAL BRITISH SOURCES

Behrens, C. B. A., *Merchant Shipping and the Demands of War*. HMSO and Longmans.

Bowen, F. C., *The Flag of the Southern Cross*. Shaw Savill and Albion Company.

Bryant, Sir Arthur, *Turn of the Tide*. Collins.

Churchill, Sir Winston, *The Second World War*. Cassell.

Connell, John, *Auchinleck*. Cassell.

Cunningham of Hyndhope, Admiral of the Fleet the Viscount, *A Sailor's Odyssey*. Hutchinson.

Hinsley, F. M., *Command of the Sea*. Christophers. *Hitler's Strategy*. Oxford University Press.

James, Sir William W. *The British Navies in the Second World War*. Longman.

Kennedy, Major-General Sir John, *The Business of War*. Hutchinson.

Lloyd, Air Vice-Marshal Sir Hugh P., *Briefed to Attack*. Hodder.

Lucas, W. L., *Eagle Fleet*. Weidenfeld and Nicholson.

Mars, Alastair, *Unbroken*. Muller.

Max, Oliver, ARL, *Malta Besieged*. Hutchinson.

Puleston, W. D., *Influence of Sea Power in World War II*. Oxford University Press.

Richards, Dennis and Hillary St George Saunders, *Royal Air Force 1939–1945*. HMSO.

Roskill, Captain S. W., *The War at Sea*. HMSO.

Vian, Admiral of the Fleet Sir Philip, *Action This Day*. Muller.

Official Log of SS *Ohio*.

Supplement to the London Gazette, *Operation Pedestal*. 10 May 1948.

The Air Battle of Malta. HMSO.
The Naval History of the Second World War: *Selected Convoy (Mediterranean) 1941–1942.* Admiralty.
The Times of Malta and Sunday Times Malta.

PRINCIPAL FOREIGN SOURCES

Abshagen, K. H., *Canaris: Patriot and World Citizen.* Hutchinson.
Bandini, Franco, *Non Volemmo Prendere Malta.* Periodical Europeo (Oct. and Nov. 1956).
Bragadin, Commander M. A., *L'Oddissea di un Merino.* Periodical Revista Marrittima (Sept.–Dec. 1951: Jan.–Feb. 1952).
Busch, H., *U-Boats at War.* Putnam.
Ciano, Count, *Diary.* Methuen.
Coccia, Aldo, *Submarines Attacking.* Gwyer.
de Belot, Raymond, *The Struggle for the Mediterranean.* Oxford University Press.
Giamberardino, O. di, *La Marina nella Tragedia Nazionale.* Roma.
Hart, B. H. Liddell (Editor), *Rommel Papers.* Collins.
Kesselring, Field-Marshal, *Memoires.* Kimber.
Martienssen, Anthony, *Hitler and His Admirals.* Secker and Warburg.
Ruge, Vice-Admiral Friedrich, *Sea Warfare 1939–1945.* Cassell.
Schmidt, Heinz Warner, *With Rommel in the Desert.* Harrap.
Weichold, Vice-Admiral Eberhard, *War in the Mediterranean.* Admiralty.
Young, Desmond, *Rommel.* Collins.
Zara, Alberto da, *Pelle D'Ammiraglio.* Mondadori.
Brassey's Naval Annual 1948: *Fuehrer Conferences on Naval Affairs.*
US Naval Institute. *The Italian Fleet in the Second World War.*

Fontana Paperbacks
Non-fiction

Fontana is a leading paperback publisher of non-fiction. Below are some recent titles.

- [ ] All the King's Men *Robert Marshall* £3.50
- [ ] War Papers *Virgil Pomfret* £10.95
- [ ] The Boys and the Butterflies *James Birdsall* £2.95
- [ ] Pursuit *Ludovic Kennedy* £3.95
- [ ] Malta Convoy *Shankland and Hunter* £2.95
- [ ] We Die Alone *David Howarth* £2.95
- [ ] The Bridge on the River Kwai *Pierre Boulle* £2.95
- [ ] Carve Her Name With Pride *R. J. Minney* £2.95
- [ ] The Tunnel *Eric Williams* £2.95
- [ ] Reach for the Sky *Paul Brickhill* £3.50
- [ ] Rommel *Desmond Young* £3.50

You can buy Fontana paperbacks at your local bookshop or newsagent. Or you can order them from Fontana Paperbacks, Cash Sales Department, Box 29, Douglas, Isle of Man. Please send a cheque, postal or money order (not currency) worth the purchase price plus 22p per book for postage (maximum postage required is £3).

NAME (Block letters) _____

ADDRESS _____

_____

_____